Wenny Has Wings

www.janetleecarey.com

Wenny Has Wings

JANET LEE CAREY

faber and faber

First published in America in 2002
by Atheneum Books
An imprint of Simon & Schuster Children's Publishing Division
New York, New York 10020, USA

First published in the UK by Faber and Faber Limited in 2005
3 Queen Square London WC1N 3AU
Printed in England by Mackays of Chatham plc, Chatham, Kent

A CIP record for this book
is available from the British Library

0–571–22353–2

2 4 6 8 10 9 7 5 3 1

To my brothers, Alan and Curtis Lee.
Thanks for rescuing me from the anthill in Sweden
when I was four. Remember how Mom had to throw me in
the bathtub with my clothes on to drown the biting ants?
Thanks also for putting up with all my weird made-up
songs and for not ratting on me the time I tried to make
the dogs pull me on my skates.

—J. L. C.

Acknowledgments

I'm indebted to Dr Melvin Morse for his ongoing research into near-death experiences of children. The book by Melvin Morse, MD, with Paul Perry, *Closer to the Light: Learning from the Near-death Experiences of Children* (New York: Villard Books, 1990), was invaluable to this project. Another insightful book crucial to my research was Barbara D. Rosof's *The Worst Loss: How Families Heal from the Death of a Child* (New York: Henry Holt and Company, Inc., 1994). Thanks also to fellow writers and artists, Margaret D. Smith, Heidi Pettit, Peggy King Anderson, Judy Bodmer, Katherine Grace Bond, Roberta Kehle and Dawn Knight for their insightful critique and support of Will's letters. Finally, thanks to my son, Josh, and his friend, Johnny Mao, for holding a spitting contest on our back deck (research only twelve-year-old boys would do). Josh spit fourteen feet two inches! This allowed me to write Will's spitting distance with confidence.

Part One
THE TUNNEL OF DEATH

Chapter 1

Dear Wenny,

I died too. Not when the truck first hit us, but right after in the hospital. I had a broken leg and a ruptured spleen, and I was bleeding inside and outside. I was pretty messed up by the truck, and while they were trying to fix me, my heart stopped for a whole ten minutes.

I sped through a tunnel when I died, then I flew around in the sky. I'd be flying up there with you still if Dr Westfall hadn't put two paddles on my chest and shot electric energy into my heart.

Those paddles must have had a lot of power, because they sucked me back inside my body. Once my heart started pumping again, the doctors gave me an operation and filled me up with new blood so I would stay alive.

When I woke up, I found out you didn't come back like I did. I asked Mum if Dr Westfall used those electric paddles on your heart, but she wouldn't give me an answer. She just started crying and had to leave the room.

So you're flying around up there in that good place, and I'm stuck down here at Children's Hospital with stitches in my side and with my leg all bandaged up because they had to put my shinbone back together.

DAY 10

Dear Wenny,

Today is 16 October. It's been ten days since I died and came back. That's why I wrote "Day 10" on

4

the top of this letter. I want to keep track of how many days I've been alive again.

One bad thing happened while I was outside my body, but I don't want to talk about that; I want to talk about the happy part. I still have some good leftover feelings from the time I spent inside the light. It's like that good, bright light leaked into me while I was up there, and I brought some of it back. I'd be completely happy if you had come back, too. We could talk about what it was like to zoom through the air and do loop-the-loops in the sky.

I'm already starting to miss you. A big brother gets used to having a little sister around. If you were here, you'd press my control buttons so my hospital bed would go up and down. You'd want to take both cookies off my lunch tray. You'd steal my bedpan so I'd have to ask for help if I needed to pee.

I missed your memorial service on Sunday because I had to stay here in the hospital. Sometimes I start to think about you being dead and never coming back to live with us, and I have to put the pillow over my face so nobody will hear my crying.

DAY 11

Dear Wenny,

All day long nurses keep coming into my room, saying, "Hi, Will. How's the leg?"

"Okay," I say, which is a total lie. Then they take my temperature and blood pressure and shoot medicine into my IV. In case you want to know, an IV's an upside-down water-bottle on a pole. Medicine runs down a long tube and into a needle that's stuck in my left hand. The medicine goes into my blood and spreads around my whole body.

If you think I'm having trouble playing video games with a needle jammed in the back of my hand, you're wrong. Today I played Zorgon Tracker. I killed about a gazillion zorgons and made it to the eighth level, which is, like, impossible unless you're a total wiz-nerd.

DAY 11 (AGAIN)

I tried to tell Mum and Dad what happened when I died, but it didn't work out so good. As soon as I started talking about the truck hitting us and how I

6

died, Mum sat down and covered her face. She had to use a bunch of tissues from my tissue box to wipe her eyes and blow her nose.

Dad didn't cry like Mum, but he didn't look at me either. He just grabbed my bed rail and stared out of the window. With his dark hair and pale skin, he looked like one of those black-and-white pictures he takes.

I gave up talking to them. I'll try to tell them some other time. Right now I'm wiped out. I've signed up for the TV so I can play Zorgon Tracker again this afternoon. I'm going to win the gut zapper on the ninth level, then I'm going to fight my way to the tenth level before dinner, I've decided.

DAY 12

Dear Wenny,

The truck driver sent us an "I'm so sorry" card. Mum and Dad showed it to me this afternoon. The cover has pink and yellow flowers on it (girl stuff). The card says his brakes failed all of a sudden while he was going down that steep hill. He was honking for us to get out of the way. He swerved and tried not to hit us, and he is so sorry. If there is anything he can do, he'll do it.

The card made Mum cry. She yanked a bunch of Kleenex from my box and made these little gulping sounds. Dad stood behind her with his hands on her shoulders. He squinted at my IV bag and clenched his jaw. I could see the muscles in his cheeks moving in and out like he was trying to crack a gobstopper.

"I need to use the toilet," I said. Dad helped me into my wheelchair and pushed me to the bathroom. I didn't have to pee. I just had to get out of that room. I didn't want to see Dad's jaw muscles bulging out or hear Mum making those little gulping sounds any more.

DAY 12 (LATE AT NIGHT)

Dear Wenny,

You'd better be awake, because I had a bad dream. We were walking on a road in a dark forest. There was just one streetlamp. All of a sudden the trees kind of melted. A big green truck hit you and crushed you. It hit me and sent me flying across the road.

I woke up all sweaty. I crushed the card the truck driver sent me and threw it into the laundry basket with all the puked-on sheets.

DAY 13

Dear Wenny,

I couldn't talk today. I knew if I tried to talk, I'd cry, so I kept my mouth shut. I know you're happy zooming around up there in that warm light. Maybe you've learned how to do flips in the air by now, so you probably don't miss me like I miss you.

I miss you hard, with an ache in my stomach and a sandpaper feeling all down my throat. I miss you like a big, empty, shut-up, quiet space torn out of my guts, and nothing can patch up that great big ugly hole you left.

If I'd stayed dead and flown farther in to meet that light person with you, I'd be in heaven now. I'd be feeling just fine. I wouldn't have this operation scar or this pain in my leg. I wouldn't be stuck in this stupid hospital bed. I wouldn't have to look at Dad's face.

I didn't even talk when Dad came to visit me today. He played cards with me awhile, then left. I was glad to see him go. I don't like being around him right now. His eyes look like his darkroom at home. I mean, no light in them at all. When he looks at me, I want to punch his face and make him fly across the room. Then maybe he'd get mad and I'd see something different in his eyes.

Only it's not Dad I want to punch, it's you. I want to punch your face for leaving me alone down here.

I'm sorry this letter is so messy. You can show it to God if you want. He can mark it up with his red pen and give me a big, fat F, for all I care!

Chapter 2

Dear Wenny,

You're probably wondering how I got hold of this blank book to write you letters in. Well, one of the youth leaders from church came by to visit last week. His name is Mr James. I've seen him eating doughnuts after the service a couple of times, but I don't really know him, because he works with the high school kids. Well, Mr James walked right over to my bed and started talking like we were old friends or something. I thought it was pretty strange.

"Hi, Will," he said. "Your mum and dad wanted me to drop by." He pulled a chair up to my bed and asked, "How are you feeling?" When I didn't answer, he said he knew about the truck that hit us. How it shattered my shinbone and broke our cat Twinkie's tail and killed you at the same time. He said it must be hard to have a little sister die like that.

I stared at the bird mobile above my bed.

Mr James was quiet awhile. He took off his glasses and rubbed his nose. Then he asked how Twinkie was doing. I didn't answer. I mean, I haven't even seen Twinkie yet because they won't let Mum and Dad bring a cat to the hospital. (It's against rule number 5,052 or something.)

I thought maybe he'd go away. Especially because I was getting sick of looking at that stupid bird mobile, but he stuck around some more.

"Would you like to know a secret?" he asked as he scooted his chair closer to my bed. "You know the famous bank robbers Frank and Jesse James?

Well, they were distant relations of mine, so you can tell me anything. Good things or bad things. Nothing you say will bother me a bit."

I turned and stared at his bald spot, his round face and his too-small nose. He didn't look like he was related to any bank robbers. Bank tellers, more like.

He pulled a little book out of his briefcase. "I keep this book to write down my thoughts," he said. "Sometimes I write about my day. Sometimes I even use the book to write letters to God."

He read me a letter about an eight-year-old kid who got lost in the mountains. The kid wasn't found until he was frozen to death and it was too late. Mr James was really mad at God about that, but I think he should've been mad at the guide who took the family hiking in the first place.

The guide got careless with the kid. Lots of grown-ups are careless. They lose keys, glasses, kids. I didn't say anything, though. I just scratched my elbow where my pj's were itching. They make you wear these really dumb-looking pj's in the hospital. Mine have Daffy Ducks all over them.

Next Mr James read me some of his thank-you letters. Letters about the good things he sees in the world. He thinks trees were a good idea.

Before he left, he took out another empty book and put it by my bed. He said I could write my own thoughts inside. I could write to God if I wanted to. I could write mad letters or glad letters. I could draw pictures in it, too. Anything I liked. I just kept staring at his bald spot until he ran his hand over the little bit of hair he's got left on the side of his head. He went away, but he left the empty book for me.

I don't know God very well, so I figured I'd write to you.

with a no-good big brother.

The truck driver thinks it's his fault. (Remember the "I'm so sorry" note he sent with those girly flowers on it?)

I think it's my fault, Dad's fault, the truck driver's fault and *your fault too*, and here's why.

If you had been a normal little sister, you wouldn't have wanted to work on the Pinewood Derby car with me and Dad. You would have been off playing with dolls, like other girls.

Thad's little sister, Jessica, plays dolls with her friends all the time. Why weren't you more like her? Why did you always have to mess around with me?

You were always into my stuff. My toys. My business. Like Cub Scouts. Who cares that you could recite the Cub Scout Promise and knew the Scout handshake? Who cares that you could tie a square knot, a bowline and a clove hitch knot better than most of the guys in my troop? It wasn't like you were going to get a badge for it or anything.

I *had* to go to the craft store that day. I *had* to get those weights for my Cub Scout Pinewood

Derby car. Dad said Quicksilver couldn't win the race unless we used the right amount of weight. I wanted to win. Thad Stickney won last year. He was so smug with winning, and I had to beat him this time.

If you had been off playing dolls or house or whatever it is that girls do, you wouldn't have tried to go to the craft store with me that day. You and Twinkie would have stayed at home.

Maybe the truck still would have hit me when I was crossing the street. Maybe my spleen would have ruptured and my shinbone would have shattered anyway. But if you were like other girls, you wouldn't have been there on the road with me, Twinkie wouldn't have been hurt, and you wouldn't be dead now.

DAY 16

Dear Wenny,

Mum and Dad come to visit every day. They don't look so good. I know Mom's pregnant and that makes her grumpy, but she used to wear pretty clips in her blond hair and put on make-up and stuff. Now she forgets to put on her lipstick. Also, she ties her hair back without even brushing it first.

When she bent over to give me a kiss, I had to tell her she'd buttoned her shirt up wrong. I mean, Mum's a high school science teacher, for crying out loud! I didn't want Nurse Pescetti to see her shirt all done up wrong. She might think Mum was dumb or something.

Dad wasn't much better. He still looks like all the colour's been sucked out of his face. Also, he kept his raincoat on the whole time he was in my room, like it was going to rain in there. After a while he put a blanket over me and rolled my wheelchair outside. He rolled the IV pole out, too. The IV pole has wheels on the bottom so you can go places with it.

Dad's raincoat came in handy once we were outside. It was cold in the courtyard, but I was glad to smell some real air. I looked up and saw a big hole in one of the clouds. There was white light behind it, kind of like the hole I flew through when I was dead. I watched some Canada geese fly past the hole. They were honking at one another like they were happy. It made me remember how happy I felt up there, zooming along behind you. I must have been shooting through that warm air at more than a hundred miles an hour, but I wasn't scared. I just wanted to fly fast and get closer to that bright light.

I leaned my head way back on my wheelchair, wishing I could rise up into the sky again. "See that hole in the clouds?" I said.

"Where?" said Dad. I pointed to it. Dad jingled his keys. "Looks like rain," he said. I didn't want to talk about rain. I wanted to talk about the light coming through that hole.

We were alone in the courtyard, and I was thinking about telling Dad what happened when I died (not the bad part, just the good part). Then a big kid came outside and spoiled my alone time with Dad. The kid had a heavy coat on over his hospital pyjamas, and his hair was sticking out sideways. Pretty soon he was pacing in front of the flower box. Then he stopped and talked to the maple tree.

"Who's he talking to?" I whispered.

"No one," said Dad.

Every once in a while the kid stopped talking long enough to clean his teeth with his finger.

A nurse came outside and walked him back into the hospital. I was glad to see him go. "What's the matter with that kid?" I asked.

"He's having some sort of delusions," said Dad.

"What are delusions?"

"That's when you believe you see things that aren't there," said Dad.

"How do you know they're not there?"

"Because no one else can see them." Dad undid the top button of his coat. "Don't worry," he said. "I'm sure the doctors in the psychiatric unit will do their best to help him get well."

I'd heard about the psychiatric unit on the third floor, but I'd mostly been stuck in my room, so I hadn't seen any of the kids from the third floor yet.

I was going to ask Dad some more about delusions, but he was busy staring at the patio.

Before going back inside, I checked the clouds again. The hole was gone. It didn't matter anyway. Telling Dad about zooming through the dark tunnel and seeing the light person in the afterworld didn't seem like such a good idea any more. Dad might think I was having delusions. He might want me to go and talk to the doctors on the third floor.

Chapter 4

Somebody get me my catapult! I've got to shoot this IV! The stupid thing won't stop beeping!

DAY 17 (AGAIN)

Dear Wenny,

There's a new kid in my class this year, and guess what? He's here at the hospital for a bladder operation. He's a big, fat redheaded kid with freckles all over his face. His name is Gallagher Krumley.

He's had five bladder operations already and this will be his sixth.

The doctors wouldn't let Gallagher have any food today, so he watched me eat instead. It was kind of like eating in front of our dog, Bullwinkle. You know the way Bullwinkle thumps his big black tail and lets his tongue hang out halfway to Spain whenever you eat crisps or jelly beans in front of him.

I remember that time a couple of years ago when you gave Bullwinkle all your jelly beans. His jaw stuck together, and Mom had to pry his mouth open and brush his big, pointy teeth with an old toothbrush. I probably never told you, but I gave you that toothbrush when you went to spend the night at Jessica's house. I was thinking it would make you sick so you'd have to come home and hang around with me, but you must've skipped brushing that night or something.

Anyway, it was hard to eat in front of Gallagher. I could swear his eyes are the same colour brown as Bullwinkle's. I kept waiting for his tongue to hang out of the side of his mouth.

23

Dear Wenny,

It's really late at night. Gallagher's asleep, but I'm wide awake. The hospital machines all have little lights on them that go *blink, blink, blink.* And every time my IV has trouble, it starts to beep. All the blinking and beeping is driving me crazy. Since I can't sleep, I thought I'd write to you some more.

I remember when I first died, there was this velvet dark I went through before I flew into the light. Did you go through a dark tunnel like that, too? My tunnel was totally black at first, but it was a good kind of black at first, so I wasn't afraid.

The tunnel I flew through into the sky wasn't at all like the cement tunnel at the edge of Jackson Park, even if the kids *do* call it the Tunnel of Death. Remember the time last summer when you and I were messing around at Birch Creek, and Thad Stickney dared us to go into the tunnel? I never told you before, but I was really scared that time. I mean, the tunnel has to take Birch Creek all the way from Jackson Park to the underparts of town. You don't even see Birch Creek again till it comes out behind Mel's Market. No kid has ever gone all the way into it and come out the other side.

Thad spat on my trainers. "Chicken," he said.

"Am not!" I stood strong in front of the tunnel, trying to look Thad right in the face and pretend I wasn't scared. I was surprised when you took my hand and tugged me into the opening.

Hey, it was dark in there, wasn't it? But there was light coming in from behind us. At least there was until we turned the third corner and you stopped your singing and started screaming. We weren't even holding hands by then, and I couldn't see you, so I didn't know if a monster was eating you or what.

"Come on!" I shouted above your screaming, and when you bumped into me, I thought you were a monster instead of yourself, so I screamed too.

I was glad when we made it out of the tunnel and you told Thad I'd saved you from the monster dog. Thad started treating me different after that day. I never thanked you for making me look brave in front of Thad, so I'm thanking you now.

Chapter 5

Dear Wenny,

Gallagher's having his operation today, so the room is empty. It's good that there's no one here, because I can't tell anybody how I feel. They'd all think I was going crazy, so I'll just keep my mouth shut.

Remember the roller coaster at the county fair? How much you liked it and how much I hated it? Well, I've been having that roller-coaster feeling again.

I start to feel okay when I'm reading a book or

watching cartoons. Just the way I felt when the roller coaster was going uphill. Then Mum comes to see me. She looks at me with her sad blue eyes and I think about you being dead and my stomach goes down faster and faster, till I'm so sick I feel like I have to hurl. I hit the bottom hard, then start racing up for the next fall. It's like I've swallowed that sick roller-coaster feeling and it's inside me all the time now. I hate it.

I remember how you squeezed my arm for the whole roller-coaster ride that day at the fair. You screamed so loud I thought you were scared and you hated the roller coaster as much as I did.

When we got off, Dad smiled at us and said, "Do you want to go again?"

"No thanks," I said.

But you were jumping up and down, yelling, "I wanna go! I wanna go!" Dad laughed and picked you up and kissed you on the nose. "Okay, honey," he said. "Let's go."

I stood at the bottom and watched you both ride. I saw you plunging down fast. You were screaming. Dad was throwing his hands up in the air and shouting. I held on to my stomach. I couldn't believe you wanted to get back on that thing!

Now I'm stuck here in the hospital, and I can't tell anybody how I feel. I can't tell them I'm on this bad, invisible roller-coaster ride and I don't know when it's going to start that dizzy-sick, out-of-control, plunging-down and no-way-to-stop feeling.

DAY 18 (AGAIN)

Dear Wenny,

Mr James came to visit again today. He picked a bad day to come and see me. Mr James asked if I was writing in my empty book. I didn't say anything. I'm not going to show him letters about that bad roller-coaster feeling. He wouldn't understand. I'm not going to show him stuff about flying through the sky with you when I was dead. These are private letters. They're just between you and me. I promise.

Chapter 6

Wenny,

Gallagher got back from his operation today. He says he feels terrible, but you should see him eat! He really knows how to pig out! We've got a contest going to see who can get the most desserts. They always have four choices on the menu, but you're only supposed to circle one. We've both been circling all four on the menu each morning.

Tonight Gallagher got two desserts. An oatmeal raisin cookie and a double-fudge nut brownie. He gobbled the whole brownie. "It's sooooo gooood!" he groaned. His teeth and tongue were all brown, like he'd been sucking mud.

I looked down at my tray. Macaroni. Meatballs. Chocolate milk. And only one dessert: lime jelly.

Mum came in and sat down by my bed. She was looking a little better. Her hair was brushed. I stuck the macaroni in my mouth so it looked like yellow fangs.

"Chew and swallow," said Mum.

I held up a chunk of jelly and looked through it. Mum was green. Gallagher was green, too. His whole bed was green.

"Put that down," said Mum. She opened my milk box for me. "I'll get you a straw," she said.

While Mom was gone, I pressed my meatballs down with my fork till they looked like fake turds, and scraped them into my bedpan.

Mum came back in with the straw and saw my bedpan. "Oh," she said. She hurried off to the bathroom and flushed my meatballs down the toilet. Gallagher laughed so hard he got orange juice up his nose.

DAY 19 (LATE AT NIGHT)

Dear Wenny,

Beep! Beep! Beep! My IV is going off all the time! The nurses have to come in and fix it about every ten minutes. I want to roll the stupid IV pole down the hall. I want to pick it up and throw it out of the window. If I don't get out of this stupid hospital soon, I'll go completely crazy!

DAY 20

Wenny,

Gallagher's parents come by every day, just like Mum and Dad come to see me, but it's different when Gallagher's parents come. For one thing, they joke around with Gallagher. They tickle his feet and mess up his hair, and they bring him comics to read. For another thing, they sit really close to each other by Gallagher's bed. They hold hands. Sometimes Mr Krumley kisses

Mrs Krumley right in front of Gallagher and me.

If Mrs Krumley is eating a bagel, she shares it with Mr Krumley. She even lets him drink out of her water-bottle! Mum would never do that. She'd be far too uptight about the germs.

When the Krumleys left today, Mum and Dad came to visit. They stayed a whole two hours, but I wouldn't have minded if they'd turned around and gone right back home. It wasn't like Dad was going to tell me jokes or give me any comics. It wasn't like Mum was going to waste any smiles on me or tickle my feet.

Dad did a lot of pacing and staring at my cast. Mum did a lot of getting me glasses of water and wiping down my table. They hardly even talked to each other.

I asked Dad to play cards with me. We played a few hands of crazy eights, then he looked at his watch.

Mum said, "Well, I've got biology papers to correct." She kissed me on the cheek. "Do you need anything before we go, honey?"

"No," I said.

"You sure?" asked Dad.

"I'm sure."

"Okay, then," said Dad, and they walked down the hall.

I swept half the cards on to the floor. The jack of clubs landed on top, so I could see his right-side-up face and his upside-down face. I dropped some more cards on top of him till his face was completely buried.

Chapter 7

DAY 21

Wenny,

Okay. This is the last time Mr Sweeney pricks my finger for a stupid blood sample! How much blood do these doctors need to look at, anyway? I don't care that Mr Sweeney wears a clown nose. I don't care that he can make it beep when he squeezes it. They're not taking any more of my blood! I'm getting out of here!

———•———

DAY 21 (AGAIN)

Dear Wenny,

Aside from you, Gallagher's the weirdest kid I've ever met. Today he put a pair of pants on his head and sang, "Underwear Man, Underwear Man. Doin' the things that underwear can."

He was singing so loud Nurse Pescetti came in and told him to take his pants off his head.

DAY 22

Dear Wenny,

This afternoon Dr Westfall came by. He wanted to show some other doctors where the truck had crushed me. He stuck an X-ray up above my bed, rubbed his hands together, and started to show off all his great work to the other doctors.

"How about showing these doctors your leg, Will?" he said. Then, before I could answer, he yanked up my robe. The other doctors all gathered around while Dr Westfall talked. Their heads bobbed up and down, and they asked him all kinds of questions.

35

"Is there any chance of his getting osteomyeli-tis?" asked the lady doctor with black hair twisted all up on top of her head.

I wondered what the heck osteomyelitis was. If I have it, I hope I give her a really bad case of it. She'd have to spend some time in bed. She'd have to change her hairdo.

"We're giving him antibiotics against infection now," said Dr Westfall. "Things have been more dif-ficult because we had to remove the spleen."

"The spleen," agreed the fat doctor with a beard. He and Dr Westfall crossed their arms and talked to each other for a while about "the spleen". Then the lady doctor asked another question about my leg, and they all started using big hospital words: "Blah, blah, blah, the leg. Blah, blah, blah, the leg." It was like "the leg" wasn't stuck on to my body or something.

I squinted at Dr Westfall. I thought about how I'd like to stick him in a hospital bed. Then I'd pull down his pyjama bottoms in front of some girl nurses and talk about "the leg" for a while.

Dear Wenny,

Gallagher has these Dracula teeth. He puts them on whenever Mr Sweeney comes by to get a blood sample. It makes Mr Sweeney laugh. I wish I had teeth like that. When Gallagher comes to the hospital, he comes prepared. I guess he's had so many operations he knows what to pack by now. His parents bring him cool stuff, too. He's got tons of comics. He was reading one this morning, and he looked up at me. "Hey, North," he said. "You ever been down the Tunnel of Death?"

I got a cold feeling on the back of my neck.

"Thad Stickney's gone in as far as the fourth turn," said Gallagher.

"So he says."

"Yeah," said Gallagher. His eyebrows were stuck way up like he was really impressed. "And Mark Johnson saw a ghost down there last summer."

"Tell me something I don't know."

"So, have you ever gone inside?"

"Sure, lots of times."

"How far?"

"I've gone past the third bend, where it's really dark."

"Yeah? Well, I'm gonna go farther than that!"

"My sister, Wenny, saw a monster dog down there," I said.

Just then, Gallagher's parents came by and spoiled our conversation by wheeling Gallagher down to the hospital cafeteria for lunch. Before he left, Gallagher tossed me a comic. "Check out the death tunnel on page twenty-four," he said.

Well, I've checked out the comic. The story comes from a real Greek myth about Orpheus. It starts when Orpheus goes down a tunnel to the underworld to bring his wife back from the dead. Most people can't go down the death tunnel while they're still alive, but Orpheus uses his great musical talent to get in and charm all the weird monsters in the underworld.

Orpheus charms Cerberus, the flesh-eating monster dog. He even wins over the Gorgons and the hundred-headed Hydra.

Hades, the ruler of the underworld, likes Orpheus' songs so much he says he'll release his wife, Eurydice. She'll follow Orpheus back up to the land of the living on one condition: Orpheus must not look back to see if she's behind him. If he turns around to check her out, Eurydice will slip back down into the dead place.

Well, Orpheus is all happy. He says he'll do just that. But what do you think he does? He walks for a while, playing his music, then just before he comes out of the tunnel, he looks back! He looks back and loses his wife for ever!

I threw Gallagher's comic across the room. I couldn't believe how dumb Orpheus was! The story's all wrong anyway. I bet the people who drew the pictures have never died before. All Orpheus does is go down a tunnel, cross the River Styx, and hang around in this murky, dark place singing to monsters and talking to shadow people. When I died, I flew. And it didn't stay dark the whole time. It was only dark in the beginning.

Chapter 8

Dear Wenny,

   Gallagher went home this afternoon, so I'm alone in my room again. The only good thing about the hospital now is that I get waffles every morning for breakfast. If you'd stuck around here, you could've had waffles, too. They might even have melted marshmallows on top, the way you like it. They do special things for you around here if you look sick enough.

31 OCTOBER—DAY 25

BOO!

Nurse Pescetti dressed up like a witch today. She even draped fake spider's webs over my bed. It made me miss Igor. I asked Mum and Dad if they could go home and get him, but they said the hospital was no place for a tarantula. I said, "What's the big deal? Igor's clean and quiet and small enough to hide under my covers."

Dad said, "Exactly."

I think Mum and Dad are just scared about breaking some stupid hospital rule. They tiptoe around my room like the floor is made of glass or something.

After dinner Mum helped me put on my Frankenstein costume, and I went trick-or-treating in my wheelchair. I took the lift up and down and visited all the hospital floors. I got a glow-in-the-dark skeleton, a vampire-bat keyring, some stickers and a ton of spider rings.

There were baskets with stuff on every floor, but no sweets 'cause lots of the kids are too sick to eat them. Luckily, Gallagher came by and shared some of his sweets. He gave me some bags of liquorice allsorts, a bunch of jelly worms all twisted and stuck together, and some chocolate marshmallow things.

So that's my Halloween so far, Wenny. Definitely the weirdest Halloween I've ever had.

One last thing before I go to bed. Does God let you dress up for Halloween? I'm pretty sure he doesn't, because I don't think he'd like the way Nurse Pescetti looked today. God probably doesn't want his angels wearing black capes, pointy hats and rubber noses covered in warts. Besides, you probably need skin to wear green make-up.

1 NOVEMBER—DAY 26

Dear Wenny,

I'm going home tomorrow. I've wanted to get out of here ever since I came. But now that I'm leaving, I'm feeling kind of weird about it.

I'm glad I'm going to see my room. And I can't wait to see Bullwinkle and Twinkie and Igor. It's

Mum and Dad I'm not sure about. Every time they come to visit me here, they make me feel sad. Talking to them is like talking to a couple of ghosts (no offence, Wenny—but I mean, you're easier to talk to than they are these days).

Another thing: I don't know what it's going to be like at home without you there. There won't be anybody asking to play with my stuff. There won't be anybody driving me crazy with weird made-up songs like, "How many pyjamas? How many pyjamas? How many are in the rubbish bin?" The house is gonna be pretty quiet without that.

I wish I could move to the tree house and stay there for ever. I'd lie on the floor next to Twinkie. She loves to lie in the sun up there and purr to herself. But I'd have to figure out a way to haul Bullwinkle up to the tree house too, or it might get too lonely up there. Bullwinkle weighs a gazillion pounds, so I'd have to get a big pulley and some really strong rope.

The tree house would be pretty nice if Twinkie and Bullwinkle were up there with me. You know

Chapter 9

Hey, Wenny,

I'm home! Bullwinkle met me at the front door wagging his big black tail so hard it made a drumbeat sound on the door.

"Get outta my way," I said as I patted his head. He sniffed my trousers and licked my hand. His breath smelled like rotten hamburgers, and his tongue felt like slug slime on my hand, but I let him kiss me anyway. You know how hurt his feelings get when you push him away.

Bullwinkle followed me around while I tried out my crutches in the house. I stayed on the main floor and didn't try to go downstairs, so I did all right.

Twinkie was in the living room, sleeping on top of the TV as usual. She was all curled up, so she looked like a dirty snowball. Her tail has this brown bandage on it. The bandage had a weird, stinky smell, but I tickled her behind the ear anyway. Twinkie yawned and curled her pink cat tongue.

Next I visited Igor. His tarantularium has been moved from your room to mine so I can take care of him. I lifted the lid and gave him a spray mist of water, just one spray like the book says to. Bullwinkle gave him a friendly bark. Igor just sat there looking the same as always. The only time Igor gets excited is when you drop live crickets or a handful of mealworms in front of him.

Twinkie came in. She jumped up on the dresser and watched Igor do nothing. Twinkie's been wanting to get her claws into Igor for a long time, but she doesn't scare him a bit. He's got that good thick glass between himself and Twinkie, and he knows it.

Mum tried not to look at Igor while she unpacked my hospital stuff. You know how she feels about spiders. Dad stood in the doorway with his arms crossed. "I'm glad you're home," he said, but he was looking out of the window when he said it, like he was talking to the maple tree. I just sat there watching Igor till they both left the room. I think I'll hang out here with the animals for a while.

DAY 28

Dear Wenny,

It's different at home without you here making noise. Too many quiet people live here now. Dad used to play the Beatles on the stereo. Now he doesn't play music so much. He used to come home from work and go jogging with Bullwinkle, or play Frisbee with us; now he just heads downstairs to his studio. I don't know what he's doing in there. He won't show his new photos to Mum or me.

I guess your dying really screwed up Dad's business plans. I mean, he makes enough money in his photo shop downtown taking pictures of babies with fuzzy footballs and old ladies holding pink umbrellas with fake sunshine backdrops behind them. But Dad used to have bigger plans, remember? He's got all those black-and-white pictures of us. Years and years of photos that he's been retouching for a big gallery show some day. I don't know if that show can ever happen now. He can't take pictures of *us* any more, if you know what I mean. It's just me now. Just me on my crutches with a clunky blue cast on my leg. Not exactly a pretty picture.

DAY 28 (AGAIN)

Dear Wenny,

I know what I came back in my body to do. I know I'm supposed to stick around here so Mum and Dad can have a son and we can be a family. I felt so strong about that when I first came back into my body, like I was doing the right thing, but I didn't know it was going to be so hard.

I keep trying to cheer up Mum and Dad any way I can. Today I made them crackers with whipped cream and sprinkles for topping, which wasn't easy to do on crutches.

Remember how you fixed that snack for them last spring? Remember how they made a big deal out of it, giving you kisses and saying you were such a thoughtful girl for making treats for the whole family? Well, I didn't get any kisses. Dad said, "Thanks, but I'm not hungry." Mum ate only one, then she made me wipe the counter while she swept the sprinkles up off the floor. I went outside and sat on the lawn chair. I ate two treats and gave one to Bullwinkle. He wagged his tail and slobbered all over my lap. It's nice to make someone happy.

DAY 29

Dear Wenny,

At breakfast this morning I put a spider ring on every finger and tried to scare Mum. Here's what she said: "That's nice, Will." Can you believe it? "That's nice, Will." I mean, she hates spiders. She

49

would never have said that before. It's like she's here but she's not here, if you know what I mean.

I thought maybe Mum would start looking better when I came home, but she still looks bad all over. Really pale and stuff. Her hair is all stringy. Her eyes are red and puffy. And she's skinny, except for where the baby is growing inside her.

She said she isn't looking so good because she's pregnant and she's tired out from work. But I don't think it's work or the baby that's making her look that way. I think it's what happened to you and me.

When Mum sits at the kitchen table and looks at me with her puffy eyes, I know just what she's thinking:

He should have watched over Wenny like a big brother.
He should have pulled Wenny out of the way.
He shouldn't have let that truck hit her.

I know just what she's thinking and I can't stand it when she looks at me, her eyes crying hard without any tears coming out.

Chapter 10

Dear Wenny,

I'm going back to school tomorrow and I'm glad to be getting out of this house. There's nothing to do around here. I hung out in my room a lot today, which was totally boring. I played rubbish-bin basketball with my rolled-up socks. Then I spent some time staring at the crack you made in my window the day you tried out your new catapult.

Things got so quiet I went outside and sang

off-key to Bullwinkle just to hear him howl. He did such a good job of howling, Mr Tibbit shouted over the backyard fence, "Shut up, ya stupid mutt!"

DAY 31

Dear Wenny,

Today was my first day back to school and my armpits are killing me! Who invented crutches, anyway? I mean, they've been around since olden times. Why don't they have jet packs for people with broken legs by now?

Kids followed me around all day, wanting to sign my cast. Even the teachers wanted to sign it. Your teacher, Mrs Fitzwendle, wrote, "We love you, Will." She even drew a little heart next to her name. How did you stand her? She wears too much make-up and smells like an old duffel bag with dead roses inside.

I hope I don't see Mrs Fitzwendle in the corridor, because I ticktacktoed all over her words with a black marker as soon as I got back to class. I also X-ed out her little pink heart before any of the guys could see it.

Lunch was just like always. They're still trying to

make the school lunch seem like real food by giving it fun-sounding names. Today we had something new: sled dogs and snow. (I'm not kidding!) That's hot dogs and creamed corn. I guess the creamed corn was supposed to be the snow—well, it sort of looks like snow after Bullwinkle digs around for a while and pees on it. Then there were the hot dogs. Whoa! They were bad dogs! Gallagher took two bites, then mushed his sled dog through the snow and tossed the whole thing in the bin.

I wrapped most of my sled dog up and stuck it in my backpack for Bullwinkle. I saw Bullwinkle eat horse poop right off the ground once. I knew he'd love this.

DAY 32

Wenny,

School's just the same as ever. At break-time Thad Stickney was his typical self. He called Gallagher names and spat on his shoe. He said Gallagher was too chicken to go inside the Tunnel of Death.

"Shut up!" I said. "Who cares about that stupid tunnel?"

Gallagher got all red in the face. "I'll go in that tunnel," he said. "Just watch me!"

"Hey, Steve!" called Thad. "Gallagher says he's going in the Tunnel of Death!"

"That'll be the day, Lard Butt!" called Steve.

I grabbed Gallagher's arm. "Come on," I said. "Just ignore them."

As soon as the final bell rang today, Gallagher and I headed across the street to Ben's Ninety-nine-pence Store. I bought a Snickers bar and a lemonade. Gallagher bought five chocolate bars and a Coke. I wanted to tell him that Thad Stickney and the other guys probably wouldn't tease him so much about not going in the Tunnel of Death, or call him names like Lard Butt, if he ate fewer chocolate bars and lost some weight, but we're good friends, so I didn't bug him about it.

I had some change left, so I used it in the gumball machine. I got a red and a blue gumball. Guess what else fell out? One of those plastic rings with a fake red ruby. I know how much you like to collect those rings, especially the red ones. I've never got one of those rings before. It gave me a weird feeling.

DAY 32 (AGAIN)

Dear Wenny,

It's eight o'clock and I'm still angry. Here's why. After school I decided to hide your gumball ring in the wooden box where I keep all my special stuff. As soon as I opened the lid, I saw that my best magnet was missing. I always put it away when I've finished using it, so that meant you took it again.

My magnet should have been easy to see because it's shaped like a horseshoe and the plastic part is bright red. I looked everywhere for it. My cupboard. My science kit. All through my desk drawers. I looked around on my shelves, too. That's when I noticed some of my warriors were missing. I couldn't find Super Droid or Master Shape-Changer or Gamma-Guts anywhere in my room. Then I went out and checked the workshop in the garage. I haven't gone there since I worked on my Pinewood Derby car with Dad.

Quicksilver was out there on the shelf. She was all shiny from that silver model paint we bought. I picked her up and spun her wheels. Slick. She was all ready to go, except for those stupid weights Dad sent us to the craft store for. The Pinewood Derby is over now. They raced while I was in the hospital. Thad's car got second place. Some kid I don't know won first prize. I don't care.

I hid Quicksilver behind some old boxes and looked around for my magnet and my warriors some more. Nothing. Darn you, Wenny! You take my things all the time and you never put them back! Tomorrow I'll have to go snooping around in your room. I haven't been in there since you died. I wouldn't go in there at all if you didn't keep taking my stuff!

DAY 33

Dear Wenny,

The weirdest thing just happened. I was in the hallway, getting ready to go into your room to look for my magnet, and I knocked on your door. I mean, it's always been a family rule ever since I can remem-

ber to knock on someone's door before going into
their room. So I guess I did it out of habit.

Dad stepped into the hall and saw me knocking
on your door. My throat got all scratchy, like I'd
swallowed playground gravel. "Sorry," I croaked.

Dad just stood there chewing on nothing. I
could see his jaw muscles getting all tight. The hall
light glinted off his glasses, so it looked like his
eyeballs were on fire.

DAY 33 (AGAIN)

Dear Wenny,

It's strange to think it's been thirty-three days
since the accident and this is the first time I've gone
in your room. I guess I've been avoiding it, but then
so has everyone else around here.

It was hard getting around on my crutches with
all your junk on the floor. I found Master Shape-
Changer and Super Droid on the rug by your
dresser. Then I spotted Gamma-Guts sticking out
from under Brenda's pink ball gown. What was he
doing in girl's clothes? I tore the gown off and threw

it under your bed. That's when I smelled Gamma-Guts's plastic hair. What kind of perfume did you put on him, anyway? I'll have to coat Gamma-Guts with some of Dad's aftershave or rub him around on Bullwinkle's back to get that stink out!

I put Gamma-Guts by the door with the other warriors. Then I saw something red sticking out from under your pillow. I thought it might be my magnet, so I checked it out. It was just a pair of heart-shaped sunglasses.

Your teddy bear, Milton, was lying on top of your covers. I gave him a pat. There was stuffing coming out of his armpit, and toilet paper wrapped around his arm where you were trying to make him feel better. I remember when you put that toilet paper on him. You spread toothpaste on his hurt spot to ease his pain, and you said he'd be in bear hospital for at least a week. Maybe you felt bad for Milton because you were the one who tore his arm in the first place.

While I was poking around your toy shelf for my magnet, Twinkie and Bullwinkle came into your room. Twinkie had the kitty snake in her mouth. You know the one full of catnip and peanut shells we made out of Dad's old sock last summer? She was having a good time with her toy until Bullwinkle took it away. He growled and shook the kitty snake back and forth. I grabbed the snake's tail. "Come on. Let go, you dumb dog!" I tugged hard. Peanut shells and catnip went flying everywhere.

By now Twinkie was hissing and her white fur was sticking up on her back.

"Put it down, stupid!" I yelled.

Dad came out of the study and stood in your doorway.

"What's going on?" he said. "What are you doing in here?"

"I'm looking for some stuff," I said. Then Mum came down the hall with a stack of science papers. She saw the peanut shells all over the floor. "What a mess!" she said.

"Get these animals out of here," said Dad.

"Wenny took my best magnet," I said. "I still haven't been able to—"

"William North!" said Dad. He said my name, but he wasn't looking at me. He was looking at Milton, with all that toilet paper wrapped around his arm. He crossed his arms and took deep breaths, like he was about to jump into a swimming pool.

"I'll get Twinkie," said Mum.

"Come on, you dumb mutt," I said. Bullwinkle followed me down the hall to my room.

Now I can hear Mum vacuuming up the catnip. I don't know where Dad is, and I don't care. I'm stuck in my room with six warriors and no magnet and it's all your fault.

School started pretty well. We even had pizza for lunch. But something happened in the last half hour of the day in art. Mrs Terwilliger came up with the dumbest project in the history of dumb school projects.

First she unloaded a pile of baby-name books on the front table. Tons of 'em. With pictures of real babies on the covers. The babies were mostly naked, except for their nappies. Mrs Terwilliger's a pretty good teacher, but sometimes she goes too far. She made us get into small groups and look up our names. Then we were supposed to draw pictures that showed what our names meant.

Thad, Kamila and Gallagher were in my group. Thad, whose name means "courageous", drew a picture of himself down inside the Tunnel of Death fighting a big, scary ghost with a silver sword. I don't think you can kill ghosts with swords, since they're already dead, but I didn't say anything.

Kamila drew the best picture she could of herself, which wasn't really all that good. She made her face a lot prettier than she really is and her hair much longer. Her name means "the perfect one". Can you believe that? I've got to tell you, Wenny, I've seen "the perfect one" pick her nose and stick the bogeys under her desk when she thought nobody was looking. Kamila's got a long way to go.

Gallagher's name means "eager helper." He spent a long time trying to decide whether to use burnt orange or just plain red for his hair. Then he bent over his paper and got to work. When he finished drawing, he wrote the words "eager helper" next to a picture of himself handing me my crutches. The picture made me feel all sweaty in the armpits, but I didn't say anything.

I looked up my name. Will—short for William. It means "fierce protector". I wrote my name on the paper, but I couldn't think of anything to draw. I sharpened the brown crayon with my fingernail until there was a load of brown wax stuff under my nail. I looked at the clock. Eight more minutes and school would be over. I should hurry up and draw.

Mrs Terwilliger came over and breathed down

my neck for a while. "Fierce protector," she said. "That fits you, Will."

I started shaking like I was cold or something, except I wasn't cold. I wanted her to go away quickly, but she just kept leaning over my desk breathing on me. "Have you ever rescued an animal that was hurt? You could draw that."

I thought about Bullwinkle. I could never rescue him from anything, because he weighs about six zillion pounds. I picked up a purple crayon and started peeling the paper off it. Mrs Terwilliger squatted down next to my desk and leaned so close to me I could smell her perfume.

"Fierce protector," she said again. By now everybody in the whole world was staring at me. I knew just what they were all thinking, too: *Fierce protector. Right! He really protected his sister. He pushed her out of the way of that truck. Yeah, he saved his little sister's life. Like, right.*

The last bell rang, and something went off inside my head. I dumped the basket of crayons into Mrs Terwilliger's lap, grabbed my crutches, and headed out of the door. I hobbled across the playground as fast as I could on my stupid crutches. I was out of the gate and down the street by the time Gallagher caught up with me and grabbed my shirt. "Mrs Terwilliger wants you to come back to class."

"School's finished!" I yelled. "Let go of my shirt!"

"No way, North. She sent me out to get you. She's worried about you."

"Who cares?" I looked around. Everyone was already out on the playground or passing us on the street. I didn't have to go back in. School was over for the day.

Gallagher grabbed my crutch and tried to yank it away from me. I held on tight. "Let go, Krumley!"

"Make me, North!"

"If I wasn't in this stupid cast, you never would have caught me!"

"Would too!"

"Would not, Fatso!"

Gallagher let go of the crutch. His sweaty hair was sticking to his forehead. "Okay, North! *Don't* go back in. I hope you get a week's detention!" Then he took off down the street.

I'm back home now Mrs. Terwilliger will have to give me an F for that assignment. I don't care what she says. I'm not drawing any stupid name picture. Not now. Not ever!

DAY 34 (AGAIN)

Wenny,

We had chicken, rice and Brussels sprouts for dinner. Barf. Mum wasn't talking to Dad. Dad wasn't talking to Mum. I wasn't talking to Mum or Dad. I didn't know until now how much of the talking you used to do around here. You'd say dumb things like, "Who made this pickle?" or "What colour is God's hair?" or "How do cows feel about ice cream?" Dumb. I mean, really dumb. Not even funny.

Dad would just about die laughing. Pretty soon we'd all be laughing. Bullwinkle would run around the table knocking forks on the floor with his big, bushy tail.

Things are really different around here now. It's so quiet you can hear that little gulping sound Dad makes when he drinks his milk. You can hear all the forks clinking on the plates.

I was getting sick of that clinking sound, so I decided to tell a joke and maybe get a smile out of Dad.

"What did the happy ghost say to the sad ghost?"

I looked at Mum and Dad. Dad blinked. Mum stopped chewing.

"Keep your spirits up," I said.

Mum put down her fork.

"Keep your spirits up. Get it? Ghosts? Spirits?"

Dad scooted back his chair. "Go to your room, Will!"

"What? What'd I do?"

"Go!" He pointed to the hall like I didn't know where my room was. I went to my room and slammed the door.

So here I am in my room. Typical. You used to make Mum and Dad laugh without even trying. I tell one joke about some ghosts, and I get sent away from the table. I'm going to lock myself in my room and eat peanut-butter sandwiches for the rest of my life. I'll never eat another dinner with them again!

DAY 35

Wenny,

You always knew how to get away with stuff. Dad hardly got mad at you at all the day you tried out your new catapult and cracked my window. Did you know water leaks into my room from that crack every time it rains? Or how about the time when you drank pickled-onion juice and barfed all over the kitchen floor? How come Mum and Dad made *me* clean up the mess? Okay, I unscrewed the lid for you, but you were the one who said you could drink the whole jar.

No one ever thought you were bad, because you looked so cute. Your little round face and curly blond hair had the grown-ups completely fooled. You even fooled old-lady strangers at the supermarket. They'd pat your head and say, "Oh, what an angel!" You'd smile up at them. They'd practically swoon when they saw your dimples. Mum would look at you and smile so wide her teeth would practically fall out.

You had everybody tricked, especially Dad. If you ate all the cookies or spilled orange juice all over the floor, you'd just work up a few tears and ask to sit on Dad's lap. All the anger would go out of his face when he saw your tears. He'd sit in the big stuffed chair. Pretty soon he'd be reading you a story or tickling your tummy till you giggled.

I tried your trick one time after I broke a glass. I said I was sorry. I even cried a little and asked to sit with Dad. He shoved a broom in my hand and said, "Clean up this mess and don't be such a crybaby."

I didn't get tickles. I didn't get stories. I got a broom.

DAY 36

Guess what, Wenny?

I just found out Mrs Terwilliger ratted on me for dumping those crayons on her lap. She called home and said she was worried about me. She thinks I need help. Now Mum and Dad have made an appointment with Mr James. You know, the guy who visited me at the hospital a couple of times? It turns out he's more than just a guy who teaches the high school kids and eats glazed doughnuts at church. Mr James works at the Family Counselling Centre in town. Now I know why Mum and Dad wanted him to come and see me at the hospital. Pretty sneaky of them.

Mum and Dad want me to go to his office and talk about what happened at school. Why can't people just leave me alone for once?

Chapter 12

Dear Wenny,

After school Mum drove me to the Family Counselling Centre. I was feeling pretty nervous about seeing Mr. James again. I was thinking if he tested me and told Mum and Dad I was crazy, I'd end up on the third floor of Children's Hospital, sharing a room with the kid who talks to trees. I decided if I didn't want to watch some kid brushing his teeth with his finger all day, I'd better act totally normal no matter what Mr James said.

We got to the counselling centre on time, but Mr. James made us sit in his waiting room for half a million years. There wasn't anything to do but make farting noises or fake a heart attack. But Gallagher wasn't there to laugh, so I grabbed a nature magazine and read about llamas. Did you know that llamas have two kinds of spit? They have a regular spit for other llamas that isn't very bad. Then they have this special kind of stinky green stuff just for enemies and dumb people who annoy them.

I didn't get to finish the article because Mr James called Mum and me into his office. He talked with Mum for a minute like I wasn't even there, then she went back to the waiting room.

The first thing Mr James did was ask me why I dumped the crayons in Mrs Terwilliger's lap.

"It was an accident," I said.

He raised his puffy eyebrows above his glasses. "So you didn't mind the name assignment?"

"Nope."

"I looked up your name," he said. "It's not as bad as mine."

"What does your name mean?"

"Calvin means 'bald'."

"You're kidding," I said. "Your parents must have been psychic or something."

He smiled and ran his hand over his shiny head. "So," he said. "Did Mrs Terwilliger say something that upset you, Will?"

"No." I stood my crutch up and spun it around.

Mr James fiddled with his pencils. He's got seventeen coloured pencils sticking out of a Daffy Duck cup. I counted.

"Did you ever use the blank book I gave you?" he asked.

"No," I said. I know it was a lie, but I didn't want to tell him about your letters. They're just between you and me.

"You don't have to write in it," he said. "You can just draw pictures. Whatever you like."

I traced Gallagher's picture of Godzilla on my cast.

"How have things been going at home?" asked Mr James.

All his questions were making my insides squirmy, like I'd eaten Igor's mealworms by mistake. I knew I had to be really careful with my answers. I mean, if I told him how bad it is at home—how the air in the house feels like it weighs a thousand pounds, how I'm angry with Mum and Dad for being so sad, how you totally screwed up my life by dying—what would happen then? I'd be locked up in some padded room on the third floor for sure. So I said, "It's different at home."

"How?" he asked.

My heart was pounding like I'd just done the hundred metres. I took a slow breath and stared at his ear. There was a tuft of hair growing out of it. Some people get hair in all the wrong spots.

"Just different," I said.

He asked if I'd like to draw a picture. I doodled around on the corner of the page, then I drew a llama hawking a big green gob of spit. I think Mr James is short-sighted, because he looked right at the picture, then he asked me to tell him about it.

"It's a llama," I said.

"What's he doing?"

"Spitting," I said. "Llamas spit green stuff when they're annoyed. They can spit up to fifteen feet."

"Wow," he said. He put his fingers together in front of his chin. "What kind of things make llamas angry?" he asked.

I knew it was a trick question, so I said, "Nosy people."

Mr. James nodded like I'd said something important.

When our time was up, Mum drove me home. I told her I didn't want to go back, but they had made another appointment. I don't care. I'm not going back. I've decided.

Chapter 13

Dear Wenny,

Dad won't say your name. I haven't heard him say your name once since you died. Now I'm afraid to say your name around here, so I'm going to write it ten times. Wenny. Wenny. Wenny. Wenny. Wenny. Wenny. Wenny. Wenny. Wenny. Wenny.

Wenny,

Gallagher came to our house this afternoon and we had a spitting contest in the backyard. Gallagher can spit ten feet six inches. But I can spit fourteen feet two inches. Almost as far as a llama. We used the measuring tape from Mum's sewing kit to measure the spit.

Bullwinkle was really excited by the contest. He stole Mum's measuring tape and ran around the yard with it till Gallagher tackled him. I think Bullwinkle wanted to join in the contest, but he can't spit, he can only drool.

We went inside for some lemonade, and I showed Gallagher my new book, *Houdini Escapes*. He thumbed through the seance chapter. He read out loud to me the part about how Houdini's wife tried to contact his spirit once a year on the day of his death. Then we looked at the picture on page sixty that shows a group of people around a table having a seance.

"My sisters have a seance practically every time they have a friend staying overnight," said Gallagher.

"They've been trying to contact famous dead people, like Elvis."

"Any luck?"

"Nope," said Gallagher. "I guess Elvis thinks he's too important to visit our house."

DAY 41

Dear Wenny,

Today I sat in Dad's stuffed chair reading chapter three of *Houdini Escapes*. Houdini had a pretty cool magic act. In one trick he walked right through a brick wall. The book showed how he did the trick, but he always fooled the audience. I went through a wall when I was dead, and it wasn't a trick, but that was different because I was outside my body then.

In the next room Mum had the radio on while she mopped the kitchen floor. A Curtis Rae song came on. I put my book down and listened. Curtis was playing the song Mom and Dad used to sing to you at bedtime. "Bright-eyed girl, you flew into my heart and set me free. No one could love you as much as I do, my bright-eyed girl."

I came to the doorway. Mum was holding the mop, totally not moving at all, like she was in a photograph or something. The song kept going: "Bright-eyed girl, spread your wings and fly away with me . . ." Dad rushed down the hall and flicked off the radio. *Click.*

Everyone just stood there. We were like three statues in the park. I could hear my heart beating inside my ears. Then Dad headed for his darkroom. Mum rested the mop against the counter and went into the bathroom and locked the door.

I stepped into the empty kitchen and touched the radio. It was still warm from singing.

Sunlight came in from the window and fell on the wet floor. I could see myself in the shiny linoleum. It was like there were two of me. It made me think of when I was dead and I floated in the corner of the hospital room, looking down at myself.

I felt so good floating up there. I was even smiling at the doctors working on my body down below. They seemed so serious when they used those paddles on my chest. And they were moving really fast, like they were in a speeded-up movie. I haven't smiled like that for a long time.

Now I'm stuck down here looking at myself in the wet floor. I have to hobble around on these stupid crutches. I have to stay in this normal body with two plain old arms and a cast on my leg.

It's different for you. You're up in the sky. You're flying around just like the bright-eyed girl in that song. It makes me wonder if I did the right thing by coming back.

DAY 41 (AGAIN)

Dear Wenny,

I don't want Mum and Dad to forget you. I know how sad they are about the truck hitting us and you dying. But it's like they don't even care that I came back. If you'd come back instead of me, you could have sung some of your stupid made-up songs, like "Alligator Jam", and made them smile when they were feeling sad. And if you didn't like the way Mum and Dad were acting, you could have had one of your big tantrums. You could have screamed and stomped your feet and hurled your toys across the room. You'd know how to get them to pay attention to you.

Me, I tell a joke and get sent to my room. I make a special snack for them and get in trouble for spilling sprinkles on the floor. Today I tried singing the "Barf Song" to Dad. It's a great song Gallagher taught me in the hospital. It starts with: "I think I'm gonna barf. I think I'm gonna barf. I ate three frogs with my hot dogs. I think I'm gonna barf!"

The song gets even better in the second verse, but Dad folded his newspaper and put it right up to his face. "That's enough, Will," he said.

"You should hear all the gross things he eats in the second verse," I said. "It's really funny!"

"Not now," said Dad.

I left Dad alone with his stupid newspaper. I've run out of ways to cheer up Mum and Dad up. They're totally hopeless.

Chapter 14

DAY 42

Dear Wenny,

I went back to the hospital today, but I wasn't checked in to the third floor. Instead they put a walking cast on my leg. That means I don't have to use my crutches any more. I wanted them to give me a moon boot, but I can't have one because my bone was shattered instead of just plain broken, so I got a fibreglass walking cast.

I'll write to you again later. I've got things to do!

Dear Wenny,

I probably shouldn't be telling you this, but I've
been having this weird problem since I got my walking
cast. Remember how you used to hide under my bed
and grab my leg when I came into my room? Well,
lately I've been having a hard time getting close to my
bed. I keep thinking you're going to grab my leg when
I walk past. I've had to keep my hockey stick in the
corner. That way, I can stand by the door and use the
stick to lift the covers and look underneath.

I started just checking under the bed before I
went to sleep at night. No big deal. But now it's
worse. I check under the bed far too many times
whenever I'm in my room. I want to stop checking,
but I can't. The more I want to stop checking, the
more I grab the hockey stick and lift up the covers.
This is probably sign number one that I'm going
crazy. There must be a pill I can take to stop me
doing this, but I'm afraid to ask Mr James about it. I
don't want to end up on the third floor.

You know I'd give anything to see you again.

But if you're thinking about visiting me, do me a favour? Don't, and I mean *don't*, hide under my bed and grab my leg. I'm not kidding.

DAY 45

Dear Wenny,

Our class took a field trip to Jackson Park today so we could take water samples from Birch Creek. Mrs Terwilliger made Thad and Gallagher and me work together, which was a big mistake. We filled our sample bottles right where Birch Creek goes underground. Since we were so close to the Tunnel of Death, Thad kept on at Gallagher about never having gone inside. First he called him a wimp. Then he called him a mummy's boy.

Gallagher looked down the tunnel. "I'll go in," he said. "When I'm ready."

"You'll never be ready, Lard Butt!" said Thad.

"Shut up!" said Gallagher.

Thad grabbed Gallagher's pencil and threw it in the river. I kicked Thad in the butt with my walking cast, and he fell face down in the mud. Just then

Mrs Terwilliger saw us from the trail. "William North!" she called. "Come up here now!"

Back in class Mrs Terwilliger made me write a two-page essay about why I shouldn't kick people in the butt. It reminded me of circle time in nusery school when the teacher used to say, "Hands aren't for hitting people. Feet aren't for kicking people. Teeth aren't for biting people."

Thad didn't get into any trouble, because Gallagher wouldn't rat on him. Thad gets away with everything.

DAY 46

Dear Wenny,

It rained hard all day, and Gallagher was soaking wet when he got to our house. I told him I'd make him some hot chocolate, but he didn't want any. Instead he walked down the hall to my room, leaving lots of muddy footprints on the carpet. As soon as we were in my room, Gallagher locked the door.

"How come you did that?" I asked.

He ran his hand through his wet hair. "There's

something I want to talk about," he said. "In private."

He pulled a comic out of his bag. I recognized the cover. It was the one I'd seen in the hospital with the story of Orpheus inside. He opened the comic, pointed to the page, and said, "Take a look at this."

"Forget it," I said. "It's a stupid story."

"It is not!"

"Is too. Orpheus is a loser. He could have saved his wife if he hadn't looked back at the last minute."

"You're wrong," said Gallagher. "I think it's cool the way he charmed the evil Gorgons with his music. Maybe he didn't bring his wife back from the dead," said Gallagher, "but he was still pretty brave to go down that tunnel into the underworld."

I gave Igor a spray with the mist bottle. Twinkie jumped up on my dresser to watch. "It's the tunnel you want to talk about, isn't it?"

Gallagher didn't answer; he just kept looking at the picture of Orpheus.

I put the lid back on the tarantularium. "You shouldn't let Thad Stickney push you around," I said.

"This has nothing to do with Stickney," said Gallagher. His face went all red, so I didn't push him about it. "I've been reading about places in the world that have special connections to the spirit world," he said. "Places like haunted houses and old tunnels and stuff. I think the Tunnel of Death in Jackson Park is one of those special places. That's why Mark Johnson saw a ghost in there."

"That's just some story he made up."

"Oh, yeah? Then what about the grey streak in his hair?"

"He did that with hair dye," I said.

"How do you know? He says his hair turned grey right there in the tunnel the day he saw the ghost! He must have been pretty far under the town, almost out to the other side of the tunnel, behind Mel's Market."

"So?" I said.

"So, I want to go in," said Gallagher. "I want to see the place for myself."

"You're crazy to go down the tunnel in winter. The river's too high."

"There's plenty of room to walk in there," said Gallagher. "Nice dry cement on both sides. I checked."

I looked out of the window. The sky was a strange green colour. Rain was filling up our old sandpit. "You hoping to see a ghost?" I asked.

Gallagher shivered. "Yeah, maybe, if the tunnel's got the right connections."

I sat down on my bed. Twinkie jumped on my lap and I petted her soft fur. A year ago I would have said Gallagher was crazy, but I couldn't say that now because I knew something about tunnels.

When I died, the first thing I did was speed through a dark tunnel. And it took me straight to the afterworld. What if the tunnel in Jackson Park had special connections like that? What if we really could meet spirits in there?

"You shouldn't have to go to special places to contact spirits," I said. "If you want to see someone badly enough, you should be able to meet them anywhere."

Gallagher closed the comic. "Are you thinking about Wenny?" he said.

I didn't answer. I looked at the crack you made in my window. Rain was coming in.

DAY 47

Wenny,

I thought some more about the tunnel today, and I've decided to go in with Gallagher. Maybe he's wrong, and it's not one of those special spiritual places. Maybe it doesn't connect with the afterworld. But what if it does? I'd do anything to see you again, and that includes going back in that long, dark tunnel.

Tonight I phoned Gallagher and we made plans to explore the Tunnel of Death this weekend. We talked about you, too.

"Maybe we'll see her," said Gallagher. "*If* the tunnel's one of those special spiritual spots, then we should be able to contact real ghosts in there."

"Wenny's not a ghost."

"What is she, then?"

"An angel."

"Okay, an angel, then. We could be like Orpheus

89

and go down and visit the spirits."

We talked some more about our plans. I'd never been inside the tunnel in wintertime. All the rain would make Birch Creek pretty full.

Gallagher kept making these smacking noises while we talked. Then he let out a loud *pop!*

"Stop chewing gum in my ear," I said, "or I'll hang up."

"I was just thinking about the monster dog Wenny saw last summer," he said. "What if he's still down there?"

I shivered. "I guess we could bring a leash."

"Right," he said. "Like that's going to take care of everything."

fishing trip," he said. "It's not here now!"

"I'll help you look," I said.

We looked all over the garage. Then we went to the backyard and checked out the shed.

"What did you do with it?" he asked.

"Nothin'," I said, and it was true. It was *you* who did something with it, and not just one something but two somethings. Remember when you tied Dad's life-jacket to the branch above the tree house? You put it on and had me push you off the edge. I watched you fly. You stuck your arms way out and wiggled your fingers as you swung over Mr Tibbit's fence. You were flying pretty well till the rope came undone and you crashed into his rose bushes.

Or how about the time you tied one end of a rope to Dad's life-jacket and the other end to Bullwinkle's collar? Then you shouted, "Mush!" and made him pull you on your skates. I told you to stop it. I told you Bullwinkle didn't like your game. Maybe you wouldn't have fallen down and scraped your knee that day if you hadn't made Bullwinkle drag you all the way to Thad Stickney's house.

You must have jammed the life-jacket in Bullwinkle's kennel that day after you went skating, because that's where Dad finally found it. Well, guess what? The life jacket was all chewed up and stinky when Dad pulled it out. It had a big tear down the side, too. Dad's whole face went bright red when he saw it.

"So this is the way you treat my stuff, is it?!" He shook the life-jacket hard. Dog hair floated on to the patio. "I can't believe you'd be so careless! What do you have to say for yourself?"

"I didn't do it."

"Oh, I suppose Bullwinkle tore it down from the hook in the garage and hid it in his kennel!"

"No! Wenny did it! She always steals other people's stuff! She breaks things and doesn't care! And I'm always getting blamed for it!"

"Stop it, Will!"

"I won't stop! It's the truth! Wenny's bad! She doesn't care about anybody!"

Dad threw his arm up like he was going to hit me. But he stopped himself. He swore and hurled his life-jacket in the rubbish, then sent me to my room for the rest of the day.

So here I am. Stuck in my room again. I'm still getting in trouble for stuff you did, even though you're dead! It's totally unfair! You should be sent to your room up there in heaven. You shouldn't be allowed to eat any good food or play with the other angels for a whole week! I hope you get stuck on a cloud somewhere all alone. I hope you cry yourself to sleep.

Chapter 16

Dear Wenny,

Mr James isn't so bad when you get to know him. Take today, for example. He asked me how things were going, and I said, "Lousy."

Mr James put his fingertips together and leaned forward. "How come?"

"I got in trouble with Dad." I could feel something on my chest when I said that, like I had a brick in my shirt.

"What happened?" said Mr James. That's when I told him about the life-jacket. I told him how angry I am with you and how much I hate Dad right now.

Mr James didn't even act surprised. He just nodded his head and said it was okay that I was angry with you. He even said it was okay to be angry with Dad! Can you believe a grown-up would say that?

Mr James wanted to hear more about the life-jacket, but I didn't feel like talking much right then. I picked out a coloured pencil and doodled on my walking cast. I was trying to get used to the idea that it was okay to be angry.

Pretty soon Mr James gave me some paper and pulled the rest of the coloured pencils out of his Daffy Duck cup. He sat really quietly and just let me draw for a while. The first picture I drew was of a ghoul. He looked sort of like Dad, only his skin was green. He had long, sharp teeth with blood dripping from them. When I finished that picture, I drew another. I coloured a picture of you swinging out of the tree house in Dad's life-jacket.

Mr James looked at my pictures for a long time. Then he nodded. He asked why the ghoul had blood on his teeth.

I said, "I guess he forgot to brush."

Next he held up my picture of you. "Whose idea was it to tie the rope to the life-jacket?" he asked.

I told him it was yours. That you'd always wanted to fly. Mr. James looked out of the window for a while. He said he liked to fly, too. He flew a glider plane once and he liked it a lot. He said he wished he could have got to know you better, because you were such a brave girl.

That's when I almost told him how fast I flew when I died. Almost. His eyes were really green behind his glasses. He was looking right at me, and he wasn't playing with the coloured pencils on his desk or anything, but I was afraid to tell him. He's probably never been dead before, so he wouldn't understand about that kind of flying.

If I told him everything that happened while I was dead, about zooming around in the sky behind you, or about the bad thing that happened with

Mum and Dad in the waiting room, he might get all worried and make me move to the crazy kids' ward. So I shut up and let him think you were the only one who likes to fly.

"May I keep the pictures?" he asked.

"I suppose so."

"I'll keep them safe," he said.

We met Mum in the waiting room. She took me back to school, where I ate lunch with Gallagher. They served us sausages, which looked a lot like Bullwinkle's turds after he ate some of the Christmas turkey, so I mostly ate the chips. I didn't mind Mr James keeping the pictures I drew. It's not like they were great art or anything.

Chapter 17

Wenny,

I've been thinking some more about how I came back and you didn't. It's not like I wasn't having fun flying around up there or anything. Doing all those tricks in the air was a blast, a lot more fun than the Mix Master ride at the county fair, because I didn't have to stand in a queue and I didn't have to let some guy with a cigarette hanging out of his mouth strap me in first.

If you want to know the truth, I would never have come back from that place if I hadn't thought of Mum and Dad. I suppose older kids think about other people, while younger kids just think about having fun.

Having fun was mostly all you ever thought about. You never cared if it was dinnertime or bedtime; you would just keep on playing.

I hated the way Mum was always sending me to Sally's house to drag you home for dinner. I hated it because you never wanted to come. Remember the time you held on to the monkey bars so tight that I fell backwards and scraped my shoulder just because you wanted to stay and play longer?

I'm starting to think that's why you stayed in heaven instead of coming home with me. You were having so much fun. You wanted to stay and play longer.

DAY 53

Dear Wenny,

The rain is coming down hard outside, like the

sky is getting all cleaned up for tomorrow. I'm in my room with a pack of crackers and some milk. If you find crumbs on this letter, just brush them off.

I think it's time to tell you what I've been thinking. I'm thinking you were pretty selfish to keep flying into the light. You didn't stop and think about us at all. You didn't wonder how lonely Mum and Dad would be when you left them down here without their little girl. Well, I've tried my best to make things all right for Mum and Dad, and it hasn't worked. I made them crackers with whipped-cream topping; they said they weren't hungry. I told jokes at the table and got sent to my room. I sang Dad the "Barf Song" and he didn't want to hear the second verse. I did my chores and picked up after myself, but Mum and Dad never said, "Good job" or "Thanks, Will" or anything. It's you they want. I might as well be invisible.

Chapter 18

Dear Wenny,

Gallagher came over so we could plan our trip down the tunnel together. We hung around in the kitchen for a while to eat some string cheese. Then we headed for the study to log on to the Internet.

"I've been thinking," said Gallagher.

"That's a first."

"The thing is, if we want to meet Wenny down

there, we've got to let her know when we're going down."

"How are we going to do that?"

Gallagher sat in Dad's office chair and spun himself around. "We need to have a seance. Tell her our plans and stuff. My sisters have seances all the time. They've been trying to contact Elvis."

I turned on the computer. "You told me that already."

"See if there's a seance site," he said.

"I thought I was going to show you the monster-dog stuff I found."

"Yeah, okay, we'll look at that stuff first."

I showed him the cool Greek-myth site I found on the Web. We read some more about Orpheus' trip down the tunnel to the underworld. Then we opened the file on Cerberus, the three-headed monster dog. Since you said you saw a monster dog in the tunnel last summer, we thought we should know as much as we could about monster dogs in general.

We already knew stuff about Cerberus from reading the comic. Fact: he's a flesh-eating dog with snakes on his back and a dragon's tail. Fact: he attacks anybody who tries to pass into the underworld.

We thought Orpheus was the only guy who ever got past Cerberus, but there was another story on the site about a guy who tricked Cerberus by throwing him a cake full of sleeping potion. Cerberus gobbled up the cake and curled up for a snooze, then the guy sneaked right past him.

We spent about an hour on the Web, and Gallagher printed out the whole Cerberus section. Then we found another site and printed some pages about seances. I shut down the computer. "If the seance works and Wenny shows herself to us, then we won't have to go into the Tunnel of Death to see her."

Gallagher licked his lips. "I'm still going in," he said. "I have to." That's when I knew we'd be heading into that tunnel for sure.

It's late now and Gallagher went home hours ago. We're all done making plans. Tomorrow's the big night, so get ready.

Chapter 19

Dear Wenny,

Remember Julie? She still comes over to baby-sit, even though I'm eleven and can take care of myself. She used to have really long hair. Now her hair is short and it's dyed orange. She has a nose ring, too. The good thing about Julie is that you can count on her to fall asleep in front of the TV. The bad thing about her is that she's one of the worst cooks on the planet.

We had a lot of work to do, but we had to make it was a typical overnight so Julie wouldn't get suspicious. Gallagher started out the evening by chasing me around the house with the vacuum cleaner and sucking up my T-shirt. I was just about to get my revenge by dumping liquid soap on his head when Julie pulled the vacuum cleaner's plug and made us eat the macaroni cheese she'd made.

After dinner Julie went to Mum's room to call one of her girlfriends. As soon as she was out of the way, I got down a can of dog food. Since we'd read a story on the mythology site about a guy who tossed Cerberus a cake full of sleeping potion, I thought we'd put something like that together for the monster dog down in our tunnel. We didn't have any cakes or sleeping potion, but we had some good dog food and some herb tea in the cupboard.

Gallagher opened a can. I tore open the box of Sweet Sleep tea. "How many bags do you think we'll need?" I asked.

"I don't know," said Gallagher. "Maybe six?"

Bullwinkle came into the kitchen and got all

excited, thinking I was going to feed him for the second time in one day. He was nuzzling my leg and drooling all over my walking cast.

"Cool it!" I said. I tore open the tea bags and dumped the green powder into a cereal bowl. Next Gallagher spooned the Sweet Sleep tea into the dog-food can.

Bullwinkle was doing a happy dance in the middle of the kitchen. "This isn't for you," I said, but Bullwinkle didn't believe me.

While Gallagher mashed the green stuff into the dog food, I read the words on the tea box: "Sweet Sleep tea combines powerful natural herbs so you can enjoy a deep, restful sleep."

"It had better work on the monster dog," said Gallagher.

Bullwinkle started whining, so I raided the doggy-treat box and shoved a Milk-Bone into his mouth. He wagged his tail and chomped the snack down in three bites.

We headed back to my room, and I drew a map for you there. I don't think you need one, since I'll be there to meet you past the fifth bend in the tunnel, but maps can be helpful sometimes when you're going to a new place.

At nine-thirty, we sneaked down the hall to the living room to check on Julie. I was glad to see she hadn't changed since the last time she came over. Just like always, she was asleep in front of the TV. She was snoring so hard her nose ring was flapping up and down.

"Let's get started," whispered Gallagher.

I headed for the kitchen. When I got back to my room, Gal-lagher had the window open, and the wind was blowing the curtains all over the place.

"Shut that," I said.

"Wenny needs a way to get in," said Gallagher.

I shook the tablecloth over the card table. "No she doesn't. Doors and windows and walls don't matter to angels."

"How do you know?" said Gallagher. He was jamming candles into the holders, and little chips of wax were falling on to the rug.

"I just know."

"How?"

I didn't feel like talking about going through the hospital walls when I was dead. I still hadn't told Gallagher all that stuff. "Leave it open if you want," I said. I put a plate of cookies in the centre of the table, and we both tried them out. Pretty good.

Gallagher lit the candles and flicked off the lights. We sat across from each other at the card table. The wind was blowing the candle flames back and forth, and the branches of the maple tree were scratching the side of the house.

"Spooky," said Gallagher. I could see by his face he was scared. He was thinking that contacting spirits was a Halloween sort of thing, but I was looking forward to it. I wanted to see the bright light again and feel that good, warm feeling.

Gallagher put out his hands. "We've gotta hold hands," he said.

"No we don't."

"Yes we do," said Gallagher. "It sets up the psychic energy system."

I took his hands. They were all fat and warm,

like balls of Play-Doh. Gallagher closed his eyes. "Wenny," he moaned. "If you can hear us, knock on the table three times."

"She won't do that," I said.

Gallagher let go of my hands. "Why not?"

"She never does what she's told. She's more likely to kick your shin or something."

"How am I supposed to call her, then?"

"I don't know. She never comes when she's called."

"It said in the Houdini book you call them by name."

"Well, that won't be enough for Wenny."

Gallagher ate another cookie. I did, too.

"Just a minute," I said. I grabbed Super Bee Man and Doctor Death from my shelf and put them on the table. The warriors looked pretty cool in the candlelight. Especially Super Bee Man's black, bulgy eyes.

"Okay," I said. "Now she's got cookies to eat and a couple of warriors to play with. She always likes playing with my stuff."

We took hands. "Wenny," moaned Gallagher.

"Come out from the spirit world."

"That's down from heaven," I said.

"Quiet," said Gallagher. "We need to make contact."

"Wenny," I said. "I've got some snickerdoodles here, and I'll eat them all unless you come and get some."

The room was quiet except for the wind, which was singing a sad kind of song.

"You can't play with Super Bee Man," I said, "because he's mine. And because you're a girl."

The candle flames were doing a jig.

"We've got a map of the Tunnel of Death," said Gallagher. "It'll show you where to meet us tomorrow. So you'd better pay close attention and—"

"She doesn't like to be told what to do," I said.

"Shut up," said Gallagher. "I feel something."

The wind was howling all around the room. All of a sudden the candles went out and everything was black.

"Stop it!" yelled Gallagher. "Don't touch me!"

111

I heard a big noise across the table. I couldn't see Gallagher in the dark. I couldn't tell what was wrong. "What is it?" I called. "What's going on?"

"Get away from me!" screamed Gallagher. "Leave me alone!"

I tried to reach Gallagher, but the table flipped over and crashed on to the floor. Then I heard a weird smacking sound.

"Help!" shouted Gallagher.

My heart felt like a punch bag. "Show yourself," I said. "Come on, Wenny."

Then, *flick!*—the light went on.

"What the heck are you guys doing?" yelled Julie. Her orange hair was standing straight up and her eyes were all puffy.

Bullwinkle trotted around the room, looking pleased with himself. Julie snatched the candles off the rug. "You idiots could have started a fire!" she said. "What are you up to?"

"Just messing around," I said.

"Well, knock it off!" said Julie. She picked up the pieces of broken plate. "You got any superglue?"

"In the kitchen," I said. "Third drawer down."

"Clean up this mess," she said, and swept out of the room.

Gallagher's eyes were as round as fishbowls. "She touched me," he said. He sat on my bed and ran his hands down his trousers like there were spider's webs all over them.

"Julie?"

"No, Wenny, you idiot."

"Where?"

"On my knee." Gallagher's hands were shaking, so he shoved them into his pockets. "She was under the table."

I sat down on the bed. "Wenny always used to sneak into my room, hide under my bed, and grab my leg when I passed by."

"How come?"

"Just to bug me."

Bullwinkle lay down on the tablecloth, which had slipped to the floor. His tongue was hanging out and drool was dripping down on to the rug.

I picked up the card table and found Super Bee

Man and Doctor Death in the corner by the book-shelf.

"Hey," I said. "Did Julie take the cookies?"

"No, just the plate."

I looked all over. Gallagher helped, too. The cookies were gone.

"Wenny," whispered Gallagher.

"I told you she likes cookies," I said.

"But we were supposed to show her the map," said Gallagher.

I checked the corners of the room. No map there. I made Bullwinkle get off the tablecloth. No map there, either.

"Look under the bed," said Gallagher.

"You look," I said. "It's hard to go under there with my cast." Gallagher went under and came out with the map.

"You think she read it?" he asked.

"I guess we'll find out tomorrow," I said.

P.S. It's been a couple of hours since the seance. Gallagher's snoring in his sleeping bag, so

I'm finishing this letter under my covers with a torch.

Around ten-thirty, Bullwinkle barfed up the cookies in the hallway, so I guess that proves you didn't eat any. He's out in his kennel now. Julie was pretty mad about cleaning up Bullwinkle's barf, but I showed her where the paper towels and rug cleaner and rubber gloves were.

Okay, so you didn't eat the cookies; that doesn't mean you didn't come and visit us. I hope you took some time to look over the map. Maps can be hard for a seven-year-old, so if you're not sure where to meet us in the tunnel tomorrow, ask an older angel for directions.

Chapter 20

DAY 56

Dear Wenny,

Birch Creek gets pretty full in winter. The water swings under the bridge at Jackson Park and swells up really fat near the climbing bars. I peeked inside the tunnel. There was only about two and a half feet of dry cement space on either side of the water. Not much room for a kid to walk. No room to turn around and run if you had to.

Behind me, Gallagher emptied out his pack and

spread all our stuff on the ground. He picked up the tape player, the can of dog food, the chain and the map, and put them back down in a neat little row, like they were on display in a shop window. He turned the torch on and off a couple times.

"Good batteries?" he asked.

"I don't know."

"You think we should've brought extras?"

"They'll be okay."

Bullwinkle trotted over and sniffed the dog food. He could smell the good beef smell through the red plastic lid, and he was drooling all over it.

"Get outta here," said Gallagher.

I patted Bullwinkle's head.

Gallagher shone the torch across his black, furry back. "Maybe we shouldn't have brought him," he said. Bullwinkle wagged his tail and stepped on the tape player.

"Get off!" shouted Gallagher. He pushed Bull-winkle's rump. Bullwinkle turned and licked his cheek. I picked up the tape player and flicked it on so we could hear the lullaby. The lady played guitar and sang, "Sleep, baby, sleep."

"Those songs you picked had better work," said Gallagher.

I rewound the tape and turned if off. "They're not as good as Orpheus could play," I said. "But the label said the songs are soothing."

"To babies maybe," said Gallagher.

"If the songs don't work on a monster dog, we can feed him the Sweet Sleep dog-food potion," I said.

"Or we could use this." Gallagher picked up the chain and swung it around. It hit the holly bush with a loud *whack!* and knocked a dead branch into the river.

"Go get it, boy!" I called. Bullwinkle wagged his tail and watched the branch disappear into the tunnel.

Gallagher put the chain into his pack. "Pretty stupid dog."

"Yep," I said. I jammed the dog food into his pack next to the chain.

Gallagher put on his pack and started pacing, looking first one way, then the other. "We should have asked Thad to come," he said.

"Thad's not in on this," I said. "This is between you and me."

"Sure," said Gallagher, kicking the dirt up with his trainer. "But who's gonna believe we've gone into the Tunnel of Death if we don't have someone waiting outside?"

"Look," I said. "I'm not going in there to prove anything, Krumley!"

Gallagher spat and wiped his mouth. "Who said you were?"

I could see his hand was shaking, and his breath was coming out of his mouth really fast.

"If we're going to do this thing," I said, "we have to go all the way past the fifth turn. You' have to promise not to flake out on me."

"Who said anything about flaking out?"

"I'm just saying this is real. We promised Wenny last night that we'd look for her, and if we don't—"

"Okay, North!" said Gallagher, holding out his hand the way the lollipop lady does when little kids are about to cross the street. "Don't go getting all weird on me. We've got to keep our heads together."

119

Gallagher picked up the tape player. I grabbed the torch, and we stepped inside. We didn't need the torch right away because the good grey outside light was shining in from the opening. The colour went from soft grey-white to dark grey as we made our way along.

Bullwinkle panted behind me. I could feel his warm breath on my hand. I was glad to feel it there. It was hard walking in my cast with the cement floor slanting the way it was towards the water. I leaned the other way to keep my balance. I saw Gallagher up ahead, leaning towards the wall, just like me. The tunnel I went through when I died didn't have cement walls. The walls were soft some-how, like if I'd rammed against them, they would've had some give.

We took the first turn and I flicked on the light. The cold air got colder right where Birch Creek started its secret underground journey. The sound of rushing water on our left got louder, too. Like the river was yelling at the walls and the walls were yelling back.

The ceiling came down lower just ahead. It went from twelve feet down to about eight feet. Lots of standing room, but it still gave me a closed-in feeling.

We rounded the second corner. I shined the torch on the rushing river. The light jumped all around on the black water. We were pretty close to the place where the monster dog was hiding last summer. Gallagher stopped and pointed to a lump on the floor ahead of us in the tunnel. I froze. I was hoping it wasn't the monster dog.

I turned the torch on it. It turned out to be a big brown grocery bag with the words MEL'S MARKET printed on the side. A gnawed bone was sticking out of a tear in the bottom of the bag. Flies were crawling all over the bloody bone. Next to the bag was a brown beer bottle and a couple of empty bean cans.

A bad stink was coming from the bag. Gallagher put his hand out in front of me, then he put his finger up to his mouth in a "Be quiet" sort of way.

Behind me Bullwinkle was pushing against my

butt. He wanted that bone. I held him back and kept the circle of light on the bag.

Then the bag started to move!

At first I thought it was me moving the light, but I held the torch really still. The bag moved again.

My heart banged inside my chest. I'd never seen a bag moving by itself like that.

"Ghost," whispered Gallagher. I put my hand down between my legs to stop from peeing my pants.

Gallagher swayed, then he put his hand out and leaned against the wall like he was going to fall over.

Bullwinkle started growling. "Shh!" I said. Somebody was moving that bag, but I couldn't see the somebody in the yellow light. I couldn't even see his breath or hear him moving, except for the way he was moving the bag.

The bag inched closer. Barf came up my throat. I swallowed it down. All of a sudden Bullwinkle howled and blew past me. He splashed along the water's edge in a crazy rush for the bag.

"Get away from there, you stupid dog!"

A huge rat leaped out of the bag. Its grey fur

was covered in mud. Its eyes were pink in the light. It drew back and bared its yellow teeth.

Bullwinkle snarled. The hair on his back went straight up. Bullwinkle leaped past the sack and chased the rat down the tunnel, barking his head off. "Woof! Woof! Woof!" echoed all around in the tunnel. The rat squealed, plunged into the river, and was swept around the next corner.

"Jeez!" said Gallagher.

"No kidding!" I said.

Bullwinkle trotted back to the bag, all happy now. He tore the bag open to lick the bone. Then he stood on the bag, wagging his tail.

"You stupid mutt!" I said, and Gallagher and I stumbled over to give him some dog hugs.

Gallagher scratched Bullwinkle behind his ear. "Monster slayer," said Gallagher.

"Just a rat," I said.

"A big rat."

"Almost as big as Twinkie," I said with a shiver.

"Bullwinkle's the bravest dog ever!" said Gallagher.

"He sure is."

It took a while for us to get up the nerve to keep walking down the tunnel. After the giant rat I wasn't sure I wanted to go around any more corners. But I still wanted to get past the fifth bend. I still wanted to meet you there.

Part Two

THE LONG WAY HOME

Chapter 21

DAY 56 (CONTINUED)

I started to notice a sour smell coming from the green slime on the walls. I made Bullwinkle get behind me, and I walked slowly and carefully, keeping away from the river's edge. Somewhere in the water a giant rat was swimming around.

After we came to the fourth turn, Gallagher stopped. "We're in almost as deep as Mark Johnson went," he said.

"So?"

"So, he saw the ghost somewhere around here."

Bullwinkle whined behind me. He wanted to keep on moving. "We've got a good torch," I said.

"And a chain," said Gallagher in a shaky voice. He kept walking slowly. He was feeling the walls, too, like they were going to tell him something.

Birch Creek tumbled cold and black beside us. I shone the torch on the water, but I couldn't tell how deep it was. We were too far into the tunnel. I shined the light up to the ceiling. It seemed low, like the basement ceiling at our house. It made me feel all pressed in. I didn't like that feeling.

"Stop moving the light!" said Gallagher. "I can't see where I'm going!"

"Sorry."

I aimed the light ahead. I tried to let the rushing sound of the river fill my ears. *This is good water,* I told myself. *This is the same river that shines in the sunlight by the swings in the park. This river goes underground and it comes out behind Mel's Market. This river is singing a good song.*

I kept hold of those thoughts and made myself

walk step after step. But I was getting a bad feeling, and the good-water thoughts weren't making the feeling go away.

Gallagher stopped. I almost rammed into him. "We're in deep," he said.

"I know."

"Deeper than where Wenny saw the monster dog."

"I know."

"Almost as deep as Mark's ghost."

"Don't worry," I said. But I was just saying those words. I was already starting to feel how wrong the tunnel was.

Water rushed. Yellow light showed us the narrow way along the edge. We felt our way along like a couple of blind guys with a guide dog at the rear. Gallagher was walking really slowly now. The air was thick and cold, and the sour smell stank like our outdoor rubbish bin before it's emptied on a Monday.

Then, way up ahead, I saw a dim light, and it wasn't coming from my torch. My heart started doing happy jumps inside my chest. Real light. Not yellow light from bulbs and batteries. Real cream-coloured light. All soft and sweet.

Gallagher went on ahead and I walked faster. I couldn't wait to see you and the whole beautiful world of light you brought with you. Gallagher turned the corner. Then he called out, "Sewer grate."

"Oh," I said. "Yeah, sure. We're under the town by now." I was hoping he wouldn't hear the sadness in my voice. It's not like I'd been thinking it would be easy to find you.

I walked under the grate and I looked up at the outside light. A big drop of water fell from the grate and splashed against my lip. It had a bad metal taste. I spat and wiped my mouth.

I started to breathe hard, like I'd been running, only I hadn't been running. We left the grate behind, and the soft cream-coloured light faded till only my torch showed the way ahead. I stopped and put my hand against the slimy wall.

"Gallagher?"

"Huh?"

"This isn't the way," I said.

Gallagher turned around. "What do you mean?"

"It's the wrong kind of tunnel."

"How do you know?"

I thought for a moment and said, "It's not a good kind of dark."

"You're nuts, North." Gallagher kept walking. I shined the torch ahead so he could see. I was having the worst kind of feeling. Maybe it was the air down there. Old, dead air with no good smells in it.

Pretty soon we reached the fifth turn, and Gallagher stopped. "Hear that?"

I listened above the sound of the tumbling river. "Hear what?"

"Listen," he said.

And I heard it. Above the water. Above the talking walls. There was a low growling sound. I stopped. My knees got all soft. Behind me Bullwinkle dropped his bone. He started to growl back. "Monster dog," said Gallagher.

"Use the music," I whispered. Gallagher turned on the tape player. "Sleep, baby, sleep," sang the lady with her guitar. He put the tape player down on the cement floor and pulled the dog food out of his pack, and took off the lid. Then he took out the chain.

"Moonlight shining on the sea," sang the lady. Gallagher made a loop at the end of the chain.

"Baby's little boat is rocking, rocking her to sleep."

Gallagher's hands were shaking. I could see the white breath coming out of his mouth in the yellow circle of the torch.

Bullwinkle butted me hard, trying to get past. "Stop it," I warned. The growling up ahead got louder. I could feel Bullwinkle tensing behind me. I grabbed his collar. He growled back. "Cut it out!" I whispered. That's when Bullwinkle went ballistic. He tore away from my grip and knocked me down as he raced past. The torch flew out of my hand, hit the floor and went out.

"The torch!" screamed Gallagher. "Grab it! Turn it on!"

In the dark ahead we heard snarling and barking. Gallagher stepped back and fell over me. "Get off!" I yelled. The sound of the wild dog-fight echoed all around, the black walls bouncing with snapping teeth and yelping. Mixed in with the snarls and yelps, the lady sang, "Morning will come shining . . ."

"Get up!" shouted Gallagher. "Run!"

I jumped up. I turned around. I tried to run, but I couldn't see. I was moving in the dark. The dog-fight all around me. Walls barking. Snarling water. "Bullwinkle!" I screamed. "The monster dog will kill him!"

"Go!" yelled Gallagher. I felt the slimy wall and tried to run. Gallagher rammed into me. I fell down hard and rolled into the river.

Freezing black water swept me back towards the dog-fight. I thrashed and beat the water. I could feel my leg sinking. The cast! I couldn't swim in that stupid cast!

"HELP!"

"Where?" screamed Gallagher. "Where are you?"

I tried to paddle. My feet sank again and found

the bottom. I stood up. The water was pushing against my thighs. I pushed back, trying to walk against it.

"Gallagher!"

"Over here!"

"Keep yelling so I can find you!"

"North!" screamed Gallagher over the snarls and barking sounds in the tunnel. Over the lullaby song. "You can make it! Come this way!"

I followed Gallagher's voice till I felt a wet hand. Gallagher hauled me out of the river and on to the cement floor.

"Bullwinkle," I cried. "We have to go back for him!"

"He's defending us," said Gallagher. "So we can get out." He pulled me down the tunnel, the dogs fighting far behind us. Then I heard a big splash. The barking stopped. The growling stopped. And the only sound I could hear above the river water was the lady on the tape way down the tunnel singing: "Night-night, baby. Time for sleep."

Chapter 22

Dear Wenny,

It took us a long time, but we made it back home. After we tied a towel around Bullwinkle's bloody shoulder, I hid in the bathroom and blew hot air on my cast with Mum's hairdryer. The hot air made my skin itch, but it didn't work. The inside of my cast was too soggy from falling in the river. Pretty soon Mum wanted to know what I was doing in the bathroom. Then Dad came in all upset, calling, "What in God's name happened to Bullwinkle?"

I told them we'd been down to the tunnel by Jackson Park. I told them Bullwinkle got into a fight with a mean dog in the tunnel. Dad got on the phone with the vet. Then he called the council.

"There's a dangerous dog in the tunnel down by the park," he said. Dad put the phone to his shoulder. "They want to know what kind of dog it is," he said.

I looked at Gallagher. He looked at me.

"I don't know," I said. "It was dark down there."

"He's big," said Gallagher. "I could tell by his bark." Dad got back on the phone.

"Tell them to get that dog," I called. "Tell them to lock him up for good."

"Quiet, Will," said Mum. She handed me a clean, dry shirt. "You'd better go home now, Gallagher," she said. She walked over to the front door and opened it, like he didn't know the way out.

"Why can't he stay?" I said.

"Bullwinkle's going to the vet," said Mum. "And I'm taking you to the hospital to get a new cast."

136

"Later, North," said Gallagher.

"See ya, Krumley." And he was out of the door.

I wanted to go to the vet with Dad, but Mum said my new cast wouldn't wait, so she helped me into the car and gunned the motor.

Mum was really angry. You know how her face gets, all white like school paste, except for her neck, which gets red blotches on it. Her neck was blotchy the whole way to Children's Hospital.

When she pulled into the parking lot and stopped the car, she said, "I can't believe you went into that tunnel!"

"Sorry, Mum."

She undid her seat belt and rubbed her tummy where the baby is. "I thought you were going to play in the park. I never thought you'd do something so dangerous. You could've hurt yourself."

"I know. I'm sorry."

"What were you doing there, anyway?" she asked.

I undid my seat belt. The car was feeling too crowded all of a sudden. "Gallagher and I wanted to go into the Tunnel of Death to—"

137

"The Tunnel of Death?" shrieked Mum.

"Don't worry," I said. "That's just what the kids call it."

"What kids?"

"Everyone."

Mum looked hard at me. "I don't care about the other kids, Will. I want to know what *you* were doing in that tunnel today."

I looked out of the window. The birch trees in the parking lot were all still, with no wind blowing through them. Mum leaned closer. "Tell me," she said.

"A game," I said. "It was just a stupid game." I clenched my jaw the way Dad does and opened the door. I had to get out of that car. Mum came around to help me. She didn't want me walking all the way along the pavement with a cast that was all soggy inside. I felt stupid for needing her help. She's so big with that baby.

I'm back home now and it's almost bedtime. Mum and Dad still want to know why Gallagher and I went into the tunnel. If you were here, you could help me make up some stupid story. Stupid stories are one of your best talents. But I'm here in the house alone, feeling like a total bozo.

P.S. The council called Dad back this afternoon while I was at the hospital. They found a stray dog in the tunnel. They said it was an abandoned Rottweiler that had gone wild. They said it was a dangerous dog, and they thanked Dad for calling them. The dog had a sore hind leg from getting into a fight. I was proud of Bullwinkle for that.

They also said they found a tape player in the tunnel. They asked if it belonged to us.

Chapter 23

Dear Wenny,

Word's got out about our tunnel adventure. Gallagher strutted around all day, talking nonstop. He said if we hadn't got out of the tunnel quick, the monster dog would have attacked us. He would have torn us to pieces and eaten us for dinner. Our bodies would never have been found by anybody. Just our names would have been in the papers, and we would be famous for being dead.

Gallagher told Kamila we'd almost died in the Tunnel of Death. Kamila drew a picture of the monster dog chasing us through the tunnel. At the bottom of her picture she wrote, "I'm going to eat you for dinner."

At afternoon break Thad Stickney punched Gallagher in the stomach and told him to shut up about the tunnel. But ten minutes later he was talking about it all over again.

Gallagher was the happiest kid on the planet till Mark Johnson and his pal Weasel cornered us on the way home from school. I suppose Mark didn't like anybody going farther in the tunnel than he'd gone, so he made a special trip over from the high school just to follow us to Jackson Park, throw us against the boys' bathroom wall, and threaten us with death.

"I'm going to grind you into hamburger!" Mark said to Gallagher. "I'm going to sell you to Mel's Market for sausage meat!"

Weasel held us against the wall so Mark could light his cigarette. He blew smoke into my face. "Going to give you a slow kind of death, North," he said. "Maybe just burn you all over with this cigarette till your skin's all crispy." He put his cigarette close to my neck. I could feel the sweat trickling down there in little waterfalls. Then he turned to Gallagher. "On the other hand," he said, "maybe I'll start by frying Porky here. Can you squeal like a pig, Porky?"

Mark told Weasel to pull up Gallagher's shirt, then he held the cigarette close to Gallagher's belly. "Come on," he said. "Squeal!"

That's when I kicked Mark in the shin with my new walking cast. Gallagher punched Weasel on the side of the head, and we got outta there, fast!

Mark and Weasel were right behind us. Since I couldn't run so well, we stayed in the park and stood near some mums who were watching their little kids in the sandpit. We knew Mark and Weasel couldn't touch us as long as we stayed by those mums.

Mark stood next to the slide. He ran his hand through the grey streak in his hair. "Come on over here, girls," he said. But we didn't budge till Gallagher's next-door neighbour put her baby in her stroller and headed for home. We tagged along right behind Mrs Boone and made it all the way to Gallagher's house. We locked all the doors and looked out of the living-room window. Weasel leaned against the fence. He and Mark smoked a cigarette in Gallagher's driveway. Then they put their butts out and slinked off around the corner.

We ran into Gallagher's kitchen and gulped down a whole gallon of lemonade right out of the bottle. Then we had a marshmallow war to celebrate our victory over Mark and Weasel.

I'm back home now and I'm safe. I brought Mark's cigarette butt home for Bullwinkle to sniff. You know how much he likes to sniff stinky things. Bullwinkle wanted to take it in his kennel, but I wouldn't let him have it. I told him it was bad for his health.

Mark thinks he's the toughest kid ever to walk Planet Earth. I think he's no different from the rest of us. He's just some stupid, pimple-faced kid who walked down a dark tunnel once and likes to tell stories about it. He doesn't know what it's like to be dead, so he's got nothing on me.

Chapter 24

Dear Wenny,

It's really late, and Mum and Dad have gone to bed. I've got a torch under the covers so I can write down all that happened today. You're the only person I can tell this to, Wenny, so I hope you're listening.

Mr James came to our house this afternoon. He walked right into my room and sat down on my bed and everything. I started to sweat, but I stayed at my desk and got really busy looking at Igor doing nothing in his tarantularium.

Mr James tried to talk with me about what happened in the tunnel. I still haven't told Mum and Dad why Gallagher and I went there, and they've been all worked up about it. That's why they made a special home appointment with Mr James.

"May I see your new walking cast?" he asked. I pulled my leg out from under the desk.

"Green, huh?" he said.

"It glows in the dark," I said.

"That would have come in handy in the tunnel," he said. I fiddled with Super Bee Man. "Mind if I sign it?" asked Mr James.

I handed him a felt-tip pen. "I've only got one more week with the cast anyway," I said. "Then I'll be out of it for good."

"That's great," he said. He signed the cast with his first name, Calvin.

"What are you smiling at?" he asked.

"I was thinking about what your name means."

"Bald," he said.

"Mum says I was bald when I was a baby," I said. "Wenny was bald, too."

"She was?"

"Yeah, bald as a baseball."

"Bald as a basketball," he said.

"Bald as a gumball."

"You wouldn't want hair on a gumball," he said. He snapped the lid back on the felt-tip pen. "So, why is it called the Tunnel of Death?" he asked.

I shrugged. "All the kids call it that."

"Hmm," he said.

"Some kid saw a ghost down there."

"Is that why you went in?"

My hands got itchy with sweat. I rubbed them on my tousers. "I don't believe in ghosts. Not like that, anyway."

"What do you believe in, Will?"

I didn't say anything. I didn't want to talk about light people or angels. I tugged on Super Bee Man's wings. You can move them around if you tug hard enough.

146

I looked out of the window. There were some white clouds in the sky, but the sun was mostly shining.

"Do you want to go outside?" asked Mr James.

I said okay, so we went to the backyard. One good thing about living in California is that you can still play outside sometimes in December—that is, if it's not raining.

I showed Mr James Bullwinkle's house. Bull-winkle was inside. He licked Mr James's hand. Even though he's feeling bad, he's still nice to everybody. He even licked the vet who gave him the stitches, Dad said.

Mr James and I sat in the lawn chairs under the tree house. Our tree house has been so lonely, Wenny, with nobody to go up there any more, except for Twinkie. I didn't want to look at it. The wind was blowing the maple branches around, making the sunlight skitter across Mr James's glasses. He said if I didn't feel like talking about the tunnel, I could just tell him how I'm doing. I said fine. That's what grown-ups always say: "Fine. I'm doing fine."

I flashed him a big smile. I figured if I said I was fine and smiled really big, he'd go away and stop looking at me through his shiny glasses. He probably had tons of worse-off kids he was supposed to meet at his office. I didn't want to hold him up.

Mum came out with a cup of tea for Mr James. There were a lemon wedge and two sugar cubes on the saucer. Remember the time I caught you under my bed with the whole box of sugar cubes? You taught me how to put a sugar cube in my mouth, count to three really fast, then put it back in the box so it didn't look sucked on. Well, Mum still uses that sugar when company comes over. I noticed the sugar cubes on Mr James's plate had kind of round corners.

After he finished his tea, Mum took his cup away, then she went to the shops and left us alone for a while. I was waiting for him to ask me another question like he always does, but I was surprised by the one he asked.

"Have you had a chance to write in the blank book I gave you?" he said.

I stuck my finger through a hole in the plastic lawn chair. He hadn't asked me about the book since our first appointment at the counselling centre. "I used the book to write to Wenny," I said.

Stupid me! I couldn't believe I told him that! What if he asked to see the letters!

"I'm glad you're writing to her," he said.

Whoa! I almost fell right out of my chair when he said that. I didn't know what to do next, so I looked up at our tree house for a long time. There were a couple of brown leaves left; they were waving hello from one of the branches.

"Do you miss your tree house, Will?"

I nodded yes. It was like Mr James had Superman glasses or something and he could look right into my head.

Mr James knelt down in front of me. "How strong are you?"

"Strong."

"Wrap your arms around me, but don't squeeze my neck."

149

I wrapped my arms around him. He stood up and walked back and forth in front of the tree with me hanging down his back. I must have been heavy with my cast on and all.

"You holding on tight?"

"Tight," I said. And he started to climb. Hand over hand he climbed our tree-house ladder. All the way to the top. Then he put me down in my favourite spot and let me look out. We sat there together, letting the world be small under us.

From up in the tree house I can cover the kitchen window with my left hand. With my other hand I can make Mum and Dad's room disappear from the house, till all that's left is your bedroom window. I put my hands out, just leaving your window there, for a long time. Mr James didn't ask what I was doing and I was glad.

Twinkie trotted across the yard, her white fur blowing this way and that. The wind was cold but I didn't even mind, because I felt like I could breathe up there. There's twice as much air in the tree house as there is in our house right now. I know because my nose and chest tell me so.

Tree-house air is like heaven air. I breathed in all I could. I didn't know how long it would be before I could breathe that way again.

Twinkie climbed the tree. She curled up in my lap and purred. I touched her side and felt the vibration. She's wanted me up in the tree house for so long.

Mr James crossed his legs. "I wrote lots of letters to my dad after he died," he said.

"No fooling?"

"No fooling. It helped me a lot." He took off his glasses and cleaned them on his white shirt. "I think it helped my dad, too."

"How do you know it helped your dad?"

He shook his head. "Just a feeling I got." He put his glasses back on, looked right into my face, and smiled, and I knew he wasn't lying.

He didn't have to say anything else. Now the clouds were back on his glasses, and there was light shining from his eyes. Twinkie got up and did a slow circle dance in my lap. Then she settled herself down in the crook of my knee for a nap.

"Did you know I died when I was in the hospital?"

"Your mum and dad told me."

"They know my heart stopped for a while," I said, "but they don't know what I saw when I was dead."

"What did you see?"

"A dark tunnel that turned into a sky full of light. There was a light person ahead of us. Wenny and I flew towards him, but I stopped because I was thinking about Mum and Dad. Anyway, I whooshed back down to the inside of the hospital. The doctors used heart-shock paddles on my chest. And I was sucked back into my body."

I licked my lips. My heart was thudding like I'd run five hundred miles.

"It's called a near-death experience, Will."

"What?"

"What you had. Other people have had that happen to them. They remember things they saw when they died. Most of them talk about seeing a bright light."

"Do they say the light's warm?"

"Some do. And they talk about feeling full of love."

"That's it!" I said.

"Sometimes they see people of light," he said. "Sometimes they see relatives who have died."

"Like I saw Wenny?"

"Yeah, like that."

"So you think I'm not crazy?"

"No. You're lucky. You're one of the few people who've died and come back."

Twinkie must have liked what Mr James was saying, because she left my lap to curl up in his. Mr James petted her fur really nicely and she gave him a purr.

"Have you told your mum and dad what happened?"

"I can't," I said.

Mr James scratched behind Twinkie's ear. I didn't tell him I was afraid to tell Mum and Dad the whole story. I was worried if I told them the good part, about flying through the sky, I'd end up telling them the bad part, too. I wasn't ready for that yet.

"Your mum and dad are hurting really badly right now, Will. But you'll find the right time to tell them."

"How will I know when it's right?"

"You'll know," said Mr James. "Just keep writing to Wenny," he said. "And you'll find a way."

That's when Dad came outside. "William Alan North!" he shouted. "What in the hell are you doing up in that tree house?"

Mr James poked his head out of the window. "Hello, Mr North," he called. "I brought him up here. We'll be right down."

Dad turned purple. He looked like he was going to puke. "Oh, sorry, Calvin. I didn't know you would be . . . I mean, I didn't think you'd . . ." Then Dad rushed into the house.

So that's the story. All of it. I breathed some good air. I told our secret to one real person and he believes in you.

Chapter 25

Dear Wenny,

I know I haven't written to you in a while, but I've been busy ever since I got my cast off. It's been hard work just to walk again, and my leg is stiff and sore most of the time (but that's nothing new). Aside from getting rid of my walking cast, nothing much else has happened over the last three weeks except for Christmas, and that was a disaster.

Things are pretty much the same at home,

which means they're bad. Dad's still acting weird. He hardly ever talks to Mum or me at dinner, except when he wants one of us to pass the butter. At night he works down in his studio or he watches TV and downs a couple of beers. You know how he used to read stories to us? Grimms' fairy tales like "Bearskin" and "Rumpelstiltskin" and stuff like that? Well, he doesn't do that any more. I guess he thinks I'm too old for that all of a sudden, now that you're not around to read to.

Mum's belly is bigger, and her baby will come out some time in March, she says. I know that's your birthday month, but it probably won't be born exactly on your birthday, so I wouldn't worry about it if I were you.

The only other thing I have to tell you is that our picture is missing from the living-room wall. You know the photograph Dad took of us walking away from him down the path? I always liked the way Dad painted colour on to that black-and-white photograph. He painted your dress blue, my shirt green, and the sunshine bright white. He made the roses your favourite colour pink. He's painted lots of black-and-white photos of us, but that one was the best.

I don't know why he took it off the wall. There's a dust spot all around the place where it hung. And a little black hole where the nail used to be.

1 JANUARY—DAY 87

Today starts a new year. If you count just my second life since I died and came back, I'm eighty-seven days old today.

DAY 88

Dear Wenny,

It rained all day, which meant I had to hang around the house after school. Since I couldn't play outside, I decided to look for my magnet again. The first place I looked was my cupboard. Remember the day last summer when I made you sing into the tape recorder? I found that tape under an old pair of slippers in the back of my cupboard. I found my Slinky, too. The one you gummed up with model-leng clay.

157

I stuck your tape in my tape player and put on the earphones. You're some kind of crazy song genius. Nobody on the planet could come up with the weird songs you come up with. I especially like "Octopus. Fish tail. Jelly pie. Moonie. Moonie. Juicy moonie. Kiss me moonie. Juicy moon." Whatever the heck it means.

P.S. I've listened to that tape all afternoon. Your songs are great. By now you're probably cracking up the angels all the time with your weird singing.

P.P.S. I think I know why you turned out so musical. Dad used to play his stereo loud so you could hear all kinds of music while you were still in Mum's belly. I bet you didn't know that.

DAY 89

Wenny,

I've come up with a plan to make things better around here, and it has to do with the baby. I don't think I ever told you how weird and happy Mum and

158

Dad acted when Mum was pregnant with you. I was only three, but I remember how Dad used to sit really close to Mum on the couch. Sometimes he'd put his ear on her belly to hear you hiccuping. I thought Dad was kidding, but Mum told me babies really do hiccup while they're in the womb. Dad also liked to turn the music way up, like I said before. He'd read a book that said babies can hear music in the womb.

Another thing Mum and Dad did when she was pregnant with you was go shopping a lot. One time they came home with your teddy bear, Milton. I remember how angry I was when I found out the bear wasn't for me. Dad put Milton in the crib in your room and said the bear was for the baby that would be coming soon.

I probably never told you, but I stole Milton that night and hid him under my covers. I wanted him so much. Okay, I'm eleven now, and I don't care about stuffed bears, but hey, I was only three then. Besides, I was kind of mixed up because Mum's sewing room was turning into a baby room. Some of my old toys were being stuck on the new yellow shelves; toys I wasn't sure I was finished with yet. And they were already beginning to smell like that stinky powder grown-ups sprinkle on babies' bottoms.

Maybe you're wondering why I'm telling you this, but I've been noticing something strange around here. Mum's belly's getting pretty big. Dad hasn't put his ear to her stomach once. Also, he hasn't been playing any music, so the baby hasn't had a chance to dance inside Mum's womb the way you did. So here's my plan. I'm thinking maybe I should do something nice for Mom and Dad and the baby. I know they keep the box of old baby toys on the shelf in your cupboard. I could get the stuff down and do some unpacking. If I grab some rattles and pop beads, maybe I can get Mum and Dad talking about how fun the baby's going to be. Maybe Mum will smile. Maybe Dad will put on some music. What do you think?

DAY 89 (AGAIN)

Dear Wenny,

I went ahead with my plan right after dinner.

Mum was sitting on the couch having tea, and Dad was reading the paper, so I put on some nice music. I turned it up pretty loud.

"What are you doing?" said Dad.

"Making it loud so the baby can hear."

Dad put the paper in his lap. "Who gave you that idea?"

"You did," I said. "You did it the last time Mum was pregnant."

"Well, turn it down," said Dad, and he started reading the paper again. I should have taken the hint, but I can be as dumb as Bullwinkle sometimes. Next I set the Busy Box on the couch next to Mum. "The baby can have this," I said. "Even though it used to be mine."

"Thanks, Will," said Mum.

I got a couple of rattles and pop beads and stuff, and I put them right on Mum's lap. Then I pulled out Milton. I'd already taken the toilet paper off his arm.

"You should sew up his torn spot," I said.

Dad looked across the room. I wanted him to come over and check out the toys. I wanted him to pat Mum's belly in time to the music, but he got out of his chair and left the house without putting on his coat. It wasn't like he was going for a real walk, because he didn't get Bullwinkle's leash like he usually does.

I sat next to Mum. She put Milton up to her cheek to hide the tears that were coming out of her eyes. So much for cheering them up.

DAY 91

Wenny,

Dad's car is at the mechanic's. Mum had to drive him to work before I got up. He had to get there early because he gets a lot of Saturday business. Anyway, he forgot to take his lunch, so Mum thought we'd surprise him and bring it over.

A lady and her little girl were leaving Dad's photo shop when we got there. The bell on the door jingled as they walked out. Through the glass door I watched the little girl get into the car. Her mum put on her seat belt for her like she was too little to do it herself. The girl didn't look like you in three ways:

her blond hair was long; her mouth was small; her eyes were brown.

Mum put Dad's lunch on the counter.

"Did you see that kid?" asked Dad.

"Pretty little girl," said Mum in a low voice.

"I had to take a full set of pictures," said Dad. He put his hands on the glass counter and leaned into them. "I feel like I've been slugged in the chest with a baseball bat," he said.

Mum put her arms around him, but he didn't turn around. He just breathed really heavily. I stood by the door. My feet felt sweaty inside my shoes.

"Turn the sign around," said Dad. I turned the OPEN sign over so it said CLOSED.

Dad usually stays at the shop until six o'clock on Saturdays, but he left work at noon today. Mum drove us all back home. I had to grab Dad's lunch off the counter because he forgot it again.

Now it's five o'clock, and Dad's still in bed. He didn't eat any of his lunch. Mum said I could have his sandwich, but I didn't want to eat something Dad made for himself. I don't like tuna anyway.

Chapter 26

Dear Wenny,

It's been a week since I got out the baby toys. I think it gave Mum some ideas, because today something happened. I was messing around with a lump of modelling clay in my room when I heard noises coming from your room. The kind of sounds I used to hear when you were getting busy with your toys. It scared me. I don't know why. Like you were in there or something. I tiptoed down the hall and peeked in at Mum.

She was wearing one of Dad's old gardening shirts, and her hair was tied back with a red bandanna. She stood by your window shaking out your quilt. *Flap! Flap!*

"Help me fold this," she said.

I came into your room. We folded your purple quilt. Then Mum tore the blankets and sheets off your bed and tossed them in the hamper.

It's just like normal, I told myself. *Just like any old laundry day.*

But it wasn't. Your bed was all empty, like Gallagher's bed after he left the hospital.

Mum put her hands on her hips and looked around. Then she left the room. I didn't look at your bed the whole time she was gone. She came back with four boxes. She grabbed a red crayon and wrote on the side of each box. CLOTHES. STUFFED ANIMALS AND DOLLS. TOYS. BOOKS. She stood there holding the crayon in the air. "I'm going to try to get through this without crying," she said. "I know the baby needs a room, and Wenny . . ." Her lip started to quiver. She crossed her arms and looked out of the window at the old plum tree. "Will you . . . help me?"

My hands got sweaty. "You're not going to give Wenny's stuff away," I said.

Mum picked up your heart-shaped sunglasses. "We'll keep all her things safe in a box," she said.

"Okay, I'll help," I said. It felt weird to be working with Mum in your room without you jumping on your bed, singing, "Gooey gobs of alligator jam," or showing me the place you like to hide your tooth for the tooth fairy.

I took the TOYS box over to your shelf to pack the girl stuff. First I packed the Magic Loom with some of your orange yarn still tangled up in it. On top of that I stacked a bunch of little ponies with stars on their bottoms. I looked around on every shelf for my missing magnet. It wasn't there. Next to the ponies I laid the trolls with yellow, blue and green hair.

At the window sill Mum was wrapping your shells in paper. "How come you're doing that?" I asked.

"I don't want them to break," she said. I wondered why she said that, because most of the shells in your collection are already broken, but I didn't say anything.

At the back of the top shelf I found all the baseball cards I've been missing and some of the coins from my coin collection.

"Some of this stuff is mine," I said.

"Take whatever you want," said Mum.

I started a pile of my things over by the door. "Don't touch this," I said.

"What?" said Mom. She didn't look up. She was thumbing through your *Horton Hears a Who* book.

"This stuff by the door, I mean."

Back at your shelf I found all your gumball rings rolling around in a shoe box with some marbles and a gob of Silly Putty. I was stuffing the rings in my pocket when I saw some red plastic sticking out from under the shelf. My horseshoe magnet! You tried to hide it from me, but I'm bigger than you. I'm smarter than you, too. My heart thumped when I pulled it out. I had to test it right away.

"Where are you going?" asked Mum.

"I'll be back." I ran to my room, dumped the

rings on my desk, and touched them with the magnet. Nothing. No power. My stomach did a flip.

Then I remembered those rings are just painted plastic. I ran to the kitchen, stuck the magnet on the refrigerator, and let go. It held on all by itself. It still worked! You can never take the power out of a magnet. Never.

I went back to your room. Mum was sitting on your empty bed. I sat down next to her.

"What is it?" I said. Right away I was sorry I'd asked, because she looked down at her hands. There was the round glass ball with the ballerina inside, the one Mum and Dad got for you on our last holiday. Mum jiggled it. The ballerina twirled around and around. Snow came down.

Mom started crying. Her shoulders shook and her hands went all soft. I had to catch the ballerina before it landed on the floor. After a while we left your room and shut the door. I don't think we can ever go back in there again.

DAY 98 (AGAIN)

Dear Wenny,

I'm in the cupboard with my blankets and a torch to tell you about my dream. I was pretty shook up at first, so I invited Bullwinkle into my room. He's in the cupboard with me now. He's drooling all over my stuff, but I'm glad he's with me.

In my dream I was in the tree house. The sky was grey-blue, like ocean water, and it was snowing. Snow fell on my cheeks, all cold and wet.

I looked up and saw something bigger than a snowflake twirling around in the sky. I squinted my eyes. It was the ballerina from inside the glass ball.

I had my horseshoe magnet in my hand. I held it up to the sky. The ballerina started twirling down to me. First she was her ordinary self, then she was you. I was pulling you down with my magnet. You were falling, soft and quiet like snow. Then I woke up.

I have my magnet with me here in the cupboard now, but it won't do any good. I know you like it up in heaven. You probably get to sing your weird songs all day long up there and nobody tells you to be quiet. You probably don't have to fight with God over bedtime. You don't even have to remember to brush your teeth.

You're happy, like the ballerina inside the glass ball, but I'm stuck down here. I'm on the outside of heaven.

Chapter 27

Dear Wenny,

Gallagher got ahold of his sister's *Extravaganza* magazine today. He read me some of it over the phone. The last article he read was called "World Will End!" It said the world would be coming to an end this March. All of the major psychics have predicted six o'clock on 9 March as the end of the world. Even some dead psychics predicted that exact date hundreds of years ago.

I had to hang up before Gallagher could tell me how the world would end, because Dad was in the kitchen getting angry at Mum.

I could hear Dad yelling from all the way down the hall. He found out that we'd gone into your room to pack up some stuff yesterday. Mum said we were just boxing some things up to make room for the baby. That's when Dad flipped out. He threw his hat and keys on the counter and stomped downstairs to his studio.

At six o'clock Mum sent me down to call Dad for dinner. I stood outside the door for a while reading the KEEP OUT sign that's written in German.

I ran my sweaty hands along my jeans and knocked on the door. "Dad? Dinner's ready." He didn't answer. I thought maybe he was in the darkroom with the door closed. "DAD? DINNER!"

"I'm busy," called Dad.

"Mum made burgers!"

"Start without me."

I leaned closer to the crack in the door. "She made trifle for dessert."

No answer. I put my finger on the wooden sign

and traced the German words for "keep out": EIN-TRITT VERBOTEN!

Back in the kitchen Mum asked when Dad was coming up. "Later," I said. We ate our burgers all by ourselves.

Dad never did come up for his dinner, so Bullwinkle ended up having the feast of his life. He wagged his tail in great, big circles. He was so happy to snork up all of Dad's burger. It's okay that Bullwinkle's happy, because no one else on the planet is.

I thought getting things ready for the new baby might bring us all together. I thought Mum and Dad might be able to be just a little bit happy for once. Instead it's just made things worse.

I don't care how the world's going to end. I'm just glad it's going to.

DAY 99 (LATER)

Dear Wenny,

It's about one o'clock in the morning. Mum and Dad had another fight. They thought I was asleep, but all that yelling and crying woke me up. I'm in the cupboard with Twinkie now. I have a torch so I can write to you.

I have to tell you about the fight. It's bad this time, Wenny. Worse than it's ever been before. I heard all the noise they were making, so I got out of bed and sneaked into the hall and hid behind the door.

I peeked into the living room. Dad was in his chair, leaning over, with his elbows on his knees. He was squeezing his hands so hard his knuckles were turning white. "What do you mean I'm never here?" he yelled.

"You're either at work or in that stupid dark-room!"

"That stupid darkroom helps pay the bills!"

"But you're in there all the time, Charlie. You won't talk to Will or to me."

Dad jumped up. He crossed his arms and looked out of the window at the rain pounding on the pavement. "I'm doing the best I can," he said.

"Well, I need more. Will needs more!"

"I don't know what you're asking."

Mum stood up. "I'm asking you to come back. Come back from wherever you are."

Dad turned around. "I never left!" he shouted. His voice was so loud it made me jump. Mum's face went all white.

"Don't shout," said Mom. "You'll wake up Will!"

"If I'm not good enough for you, Kate, just say so!"

"That's not what I'm saying. Listen to me, Charlie. I need you to start living here again. I want you to promise that you're going to protect us and you're going to *love* this new baby when it comes."

Dad paced back and forth in front of the window. "How can I promise to protect you when we both know how crazy and dangerous it is out there?" He waved his arms above his head. "There are murderers and poisoned Halloween sweets and and drugs. Kids get hurt and we can't do anything to protect them. Nothing!"

"Say it," said Mum. She touched the place on the wall where our picture used to be. "Say your daughter's name, Charlie. You haven't been able to say her name since the funeral. Say 'Wenny'."

That's when Dad let out this big roar, like his mouth was a cave with this wild animal trapped inside. Mum gripped the mantel. I scrunched down in the corner of the hallway. Dad ran out of the house, slammed the car door, and drove off down the street. I could hear his tyres screeching from all the way inside the house.

I waited a long time behind the door, then I went in and sat next to Mum. She put her head on my shoulder like I was the dad and she was the kid. I touched her belly. It was so big with that baby.

"Why's Dad so angry with you?" I asked.

"He's not angry with me, honey. He's angry with himself." Mum ran her fingers through my hair. "He blames himself for what happened to you and Wenny."

"It wasn't his fault."

"I know, Will. But he doesn't know that."

The rain pounded on the window with wet fingers. I could hear my own heartbeat in my ears.

"Mum?"

"Yeah?"

"We were on the zebra crossing."

"I know."

"I ran and Wenny ran too, but I ran faster than she did."

"You were older and you could run faster."

"I screamed for her to run, Mum, but the truck came so fast."

"I know."

Then I was crying on her shoulder, and I got the roses on her robe all wet and snotty. Mum held me close for a long time. I could hear the clock ticking on the mantel. I could feel Mum's breath on my neck.

After a while Mum walked me down the hall and tucked me into bed. "Try to get some sleep," she said.

That was an hour ago. I tried to sleep, but my worries got in the way, so here I am in the cupboard with Twinkie on my lap. She's keeping my legs warm while I write. There aren't many cars on the road at one o'clock in the morning. Every time I hear one pass, I think it's Dad, but it's not.

I want you to fly around and find Dad, Wenny. If you can't find him by yourself, get God to send out some older angels to help. Find him and bring him home.

Chapter 28

Dear Wenny,

I hope you're busy looking for Dad. I'm praying God gives you some angels to help you, because you were always better at losing things than finding them. Ten angels would probably be enough. Especially if some of them are guys. I'll make this letter short. I know you're busy, but I have to write. There's no one else I can tell this to.

Mum said Dad went away because he's angry

with himself about what happened to you. I think she's right, but there's another reason, too. I think Dad's afraid the baby will be a girl. He doesn't want to get to know another girl, then have her die on him like you did. I want to ask Mum if my idea is right, but it would just make her cry again. What do you think?

If it's a girl, I'm going to teach her to play in the house with girl stuff. I'll give her dolls for her birthday and a plastic tea set for Christmas. The cups will be so small she'll have to hold them with her fingertips. I won't let her climb on to the counter in the kitchen. I won't let her drink a whole jar of pickled-onion juice or fly from the tree house with Dad's life jacket on or have Bullwinkle pull her on roller skates. I won't let her play with the warriors or go on adventures. Most especially, I won't let her go into the Tunnel of Death like we did. She'll be a normal girl. In the house. Safe.

If you bring Dad back, I'll tell him my plans so he doesn't have to be so scared.

DAY 100 (LATE AT NIGHT)

Dear Wenny,

Dad's still missing. Mum has already called the police, and they're looking for him too. I think it would be better for Dad if you found him before the cops do, don't you? But I'm beginning to wonder what the heck you angels are up to. Don't you have special powers by now? I bet you can see through walls and stuff like that. What's taking you so long?

Chapter 29

Dear Wenny,

I'm sitting by the phone. Dad called and said he was all right. He said he'd call later when Mum gets home and tell her where he is.

Dad asked how I was doing, and I said, "Okay." He said he hoped I wasn't angry with him. I didn't say anything. I just played with the phone cord.

"I'll call back," said Dad. Then he hung up. I sat

there listening to the dial tone. *Buuuuuuzzzzzz*. My
brains felt all electric.

DAY 102

Dear Wenny,

I don't know if it was you who found Dad or not,
but in case it wasn't, I'll tell you where he is. He's
staying in San Francisco with his friend Jim Garvey.
Mum wanted to call Mr. Garvey after Dad left, but
he has a new ex-directory number she didn't know.

Remember Mr Garvey, Wenny? He's the one
who came to dinner a load of times last year. Mum
and Dad kept inviting him over because he'd just
got divorced and he was lonely. Last time Mr
Garvey came over, he pinched your cheeks and
called you Little Miss Angel so many times I wanted to puke.

Anyway, Mr Garvey lives in his own flat in the
city. Dad's been sleeping on his couch. I found all
this out by listening to Mum talk on the phone with
Dad. She was really good and strong. She didn't cry
or anything. You'd be proud of her for that.

Dad said he wasn't ready to come home yet, but he wants me to visit him at Mr Garvey's. What do you think?

DAY 104

Dear Wenny,

It's Friday night. I couldn't sleep until I wrote to you. I'm over here at Mr Garvey's. It's past midnight, and I'm sitting on the edge of the bathtub with the bathroom light on so I won't wake up anybody.

Mr Garvey's flat is certainly different from a normal house. First off, he doesn't have any pets, unless you count the fake tropical fish that swim around on his computer screen. His furniture is really modern. His couch and chairs are all black leather. His tables are made of glass and steel. When the sun shines through the window, it bounces around on all the tables and lands smack in your eyes so you've got to squint.

Another thing about Mr Garvey's flat it's full of grown-up toys. Mazes, 3-D puzzles and glass sculptures with blue or yellow goop that drips down inside them like alien guts on display. He's also got the best and newest computer, a DVD player and a big fat TV.

Tonight, after our pizza, we rented DVDs, ate popcorn and drank beer, which are all things guys do for fun. Even though mine was ginger beer, Dad poured it into a real beer stein. (That's a big mug with pictures of mountains and guys in leather shorts and stuff.) My ginger beer had tons more foam than normal beer.

I wanted to get Dad alone and talk about my plan to take care of the baby so he could come back home and not worry so much. But he stuck to Mr Garvey like chewing gum. The only time I got him to myself, I ran for my backpack.

"I've got something of yours," I said.

"Yeah?"

I unzipped the pack and pulled out his toothbrush. "I figured your teeth might be pretty scuzzy by now."

"Thanks, Will. I bought myself another toothbrush at the chemist's." He took it out of my hand.

185

"But it was cheap. I like mine much better."

That was it. My big moment to tell Dad I'd take care of the baby. I was going to promise him I'd live up to my name Will, which means "fierce protector". I'd keep our new baby safe.

Everything was quiet. Dad was looking right at me, and all I said was his teeth were probably scuzzy.

DAY 105

Dear Wenny,

I wish Dad weren't so angry about us packing up your room. It's not a fun job, but the baby's going to need a place to sleep. It will still be your room, too. I promise.

If you can think of some way to help Dad feel better, I hope you can let me know. I'm doing everything I can. So far, it's just been one big screw-up.

You should know, Mum and I have finished packing up your room. I took back all my toys. I have most of your little-kid books saved on my shelf. I'm going to read them to the baby someday. The only other things I took were the gumball rings, a couple of ugly trolls and the ballerina inside the glass ball.

Tomorrow we're going to go in there and paint the walls. Guess what colour it's going to be?

DAY 106

I don't want you to worry too much about Igor not eating his grasshopper today. Maybe he just wasn't hungry.

DAY 107

Dear Wenny,

We've been painting your room. It's turned out to be a lot of work. Mum let me pick the colours. First we painted the walls and ceiling all light blue, then I told Mum my plan to paint white clouds on top of the blue. At first Mum didn't like the idea, but she gave in after I told her I'd share my stash of Snickers bars with her.

I'm about halfway through with the clouds now. I'm using a sponge to paint them on. The clouds

187

look okay, but not as good as they looked when I was dead for a while. I painted a hole in the clouds with white light coming through. It wasn't as bright as I wanted it to be. You can't find that kind of brightness at Hal's Hardware Store.

P.S. I think Igor misses Dad, because he's still not eating.

Chapter 30

Dear Wenny,

I should have been paying more attention to Igor! When I got home from school, he was flat on his back. There was a crack in the side of his leg. I thought he might be dying. Mum was at work, so I called Dad at the shop. He gave me Mr Sollazzo's phone number at the pet shop. "Mr Sollazzo's an expert on tarantulas," said Dad. "If he tells you to take Igor to the vet, I'll come over and pick you up."

I told Dad thanks and called Mr Sollazzo. It turned out we didn't need to go to the vet, because Mr Sollazzo told me some big news. Igor's moulting!

He told me moulting is something tarantulas do once or twice a year. They stop eating. Then they lie on their back and break out of their old outside skeleton (called an exoskeleton). This is so they can grow more.

Since we've had Igor eleven months and this is the first time we've seen him moult, Mr Sollazzo told me some other news. Are you ready, because this is important. Mr Sollazzo told me Igor's a girl!

I said, "No way!" but he said male tarantulas don't moult any more once they reach adulthood. Females continue to moult every year through their whole life.

He told me what I need to do to take care of Igor while she's moulting. Mostly just watch her closely and keep her tarantularium moist.

I know it's weird to start thinking of Igor as a girl after all this time. I thought about changing her name, but I decided since she's your spider and you named her Igor on her first day home, she'll stay Igor.

Mr Sollazzo said once Igor's all the way out, I can take away the exoskeleton. The exoskeleton will look just like a tarantula, but there won't be anything living inside it any more. Kind of like when your angel self steps out of your old outside body and flies away.

People have to die to have this kind of thing happen. But tarantulas are lucky. They get to practise stepping out of their old outside bodies in their own lifetime.

DAY 111

Dear Wenny,

Igor has finished moulting. Her new self is beautiful, like she's taken a bath or something. I called Dad and told him Igor's a girl, and he laughed. I actually made Dad laugh for about thirty seconds. That made me feel good.

Today I took Igor's old exoskeleton out of her tarantularium. Mum didn't want to see it. But Twinkie's a different story. She went nuts with excitement.

After she calmed down, I let her sniff Igor's exoskeleton. She sniffed and sniffed. Then she touched it really softly with her paw, like it was her own baby kitten.

I took Igor's exoskeleton to school for show-and-tell. Mrs Terwilliger was almost as excited as Twinkie. She didn't want to touch the exoskeleton, though.

I suppose God didn't want us to have to go through the trouble of moulting every year, so he put our skeleton inside our body. But I think moulting would be fun. You could miss three whole days of school, and your mum and dad would have to write a note, like "Please excuse Will from school this week, he's molting."

DAY 112

Dear Wenny,

Twinkie is still upset with me for taking Igor's exoskeleton to school and leaving it in the clear plastic box on the science shelf. Bullwinkle can tell she's upset, too. I noticed he's been sniffing Twinkie

192

more than usual. Maybe upsetness has a funny kind of smell. Anyway, Bullwinkle's been doing all he can to cheer up Twinkie.

Remember Dad's red-and-black-checked boxer shorts? The ones you took out of Dad's drawer that time and tried to play draughts on? Well, Bullwinkle dug them out of the dirty-laundry pile and gave them to Twinkie as a special present. Mum took the present back to the washing machine before Twinkie could decide whether she liked it or not, but that didn't stop Bullwinkle from bringing her a whole pile of things. He brought my old soccer shoe, the paper that last night's fish was wrapped in, some used Kleenex and a cream of mushroom soup can from the recycling bin.

Twinkie licked the can a little before Mum took away the stuff. I think Bullwinkle would have kept giving Twinkie gifts like it was her birthday or something if Mum hadn't yelled at him and kicked him outside.

Later in the day I went out to his kennel to tell him what a good, smart, furry dog he is. He wagged his tail against his kennel—*thump, thump, thump*—and slobbered all over me.

Since Bullwinkle had such a good idea, I tried to make up with Twinkie. I got a nice china bowl out of the cupboard. I filled it to the top with fresh, cold milk and put it on the floor. Twinkie sniffed the milk, then lapped it up. She drank it all the way down. When she had finished, she licked her mouth and paws, and jumped up in my lap. If she could talk, I know she'd be saying, "It's all right that you took Igor's exoskeleton to school, I love you anyway." But she didn't have to talk. She only had to purr. A purr is worth a thousand words.

Chapter 31

Dear Wenny,

Yesterday I went to visit Dad. He took me out for Mexican food, and we had a hot pepper contest. He bet me I couldn't eat a whole cooked chili pepper. I bet him I could, and I won, so after dinner he had to buy me a double-decker ice-cream cone. I got chocolate marble and raspberry swirl.

I wish Dad were ready to come home, but he says he has some stuff to work out first. You should

know that Mum and Dad are seeing a counsellor at
the Family Counselling Centre. It's not Mr. James,
because he just works with kids. It's someone else,
named Mrs Kershel. Mum says Dad's been working
through his grief issues. And when he comes home,
things will be different. Things will be better.

I hope he hurries up with his grief issues,
because I miss him. I'm the only guy around here,
aside from Bullwinkle, and he doesn't count because
he's a dog. Even Igor's a girl, it turns out, so I feel
way outnumbered all of a sudden.

I was missing Dad so much today that I did
something I shouldn't have done. I stole the key
and sneaked downstairs to his studio.

You know all those black-and-white pictures
he's taken of us over the years, the ones he painted
on so they look really old? Well, he's got all those
pictures framed and stored in neat boxes. I don't
know whether he's putting them away for ever or
packing them up for that gallery exhibition he was
going to have. I looked through the photos, and
they're good. I hope he has an exhibition.

The picture on top was the one of you and me walking down the path. You know, the one Dad took off the living-room wall. After I checked out the rest of the box, I looked at the black and whites he's been working on now. That's when I figured out why Dad's been locking the door. He hasn't wanted Mum and me to see.

Dad's been painting on some black-and-white pictures of us, Wenny, but they're not the good shots. These pictures are what Dad used to call throwaways.

You know how squirmy you always were, how Dad always had to take ten zillion photographs of us to get one good one? Well, he's been fooling around with the throwaways.

The first picture was of you and me in the sand-pit. You were probably three. We were supposed to be doing a nice sandcastle photo, only you got bored and poured your glass of lemonade over my head. We had to stop so Dad could drag me into the bathroom and wash the sticky stuff out of my hair. I remember how angry Dad was. He scrubbed my head so hard I thought my scalp was going to rip right off. The thing I didn't know was that Dad got a picture of you pouring the lemonade over my head.

The second shot was of you stomping on a party hat with your dress shoe.

The third picture really got to me. It was taken on the when day we walked down the path together.

Right after he got the good photo that used to hang on the living-room wall, you raced on ahead of me. I turned around and looked at Dad, and he took the shot.

It's a strange-looking photo. There I am looking at Dad. And way up ahead of us on the path you're running into the sunlight with your arms spread apart like you're going to take off.

I don't know why Dad wanted to paint on that picture, but he hasn't finished it yet. I'm still black and white: my hair, my face, my clothes. But Dad painted your dress blue, your curly hair blond, and your spread-out arms light pink. He painted red roses on the sides of the path, and he painted the gold sunlight you're running into.

Stadium. Then he grabs a few Yankees fans for a quick snack before he heads off for a date with the Statue of Liberty.

When we finished the comic, Gallagher did his Godzilla impression. He stomped around my room yelling, "Smash! Stomp! Whomp! Hey, here're some juicy Yankees fans! I think I'll grab a snack. Munch! Munch!" He lifted his shirt and rubbed his fat belly. "Now I'm thirsty!" he growled. "Where the heck can a guy get a couple of hundred gallons of lemonade around here?" Saying that made Gallagher hungry, so we went to the kitchen for a snack.

At five o'clock Gallagher's dad picked us up in his car and took us out for Gallagher's birthday dinner. We ate at the China Dragon restaurant in San Francisco. I pigged out on sweet-and-sour pork. I also ate those crunchy brown noodles that look like fried worms. Gallagher liked his noodles so much he jammed a load of them in his pocket so he could eat more later. Anyway, it was dark by the time we headed back home across the Golden Gate Bridge.

I opened my window and stuck my head out.

The first thing that hit me was the wind whooshing past my ears. Golden Gate Bridge air is so great! It should be bottled or something. Cars were speeding towards San Francisco on the other side of the bridge. The white headlights were like zillions of shooting stars. It was just like the light show I saw when I died. Did you see a light show before you left the dark tunnel? I saw shooting stars all around me, and I could feel warmth coming from them. I did a flip and I was out of the tunnel, flying in that river of light.

I'd forgotten all about that light show at the end of the tunnel until tonight. Feeling that fresh wind on my face, zooming through all those beautiful lights, made me remember. I was gulping down so much happiness that I started shouting. Gallagher started shouting, too.

Gallagher's dad told us to be quiet and roll up the window. I did what I was told. It didn't matter. We were over the bridge anyway, and I was full of good feelings, like those bright lights were shooting through my body.

I was so glad to have heard that loud whooshing sound. I was so glad to have seen those flying lights again. It was better than the best kind of dream.

DAY 140

Dear Wenny,

It's been a while since I've written, but I've been hanging around at Gallagher's house a lot. I went to his house again after school today. We had a snack of crackers, apples smeared with peanut butter, and chocolate milk. Have you ever filled your mouth with crackers and tried to whistle? Gallagher and I had a contest. We couldn't stop laughing. You should get some of the angels together and try it some time. It's a riot. I don't think God would mind you playing with crackers. He must like a good laugh every once in a while, otherwise he wouldn't have come up with things like baboons and walruses.

March will be here soon, and Gallagher and I made some important plans together. I can't tell you our plans right now because they're secret. Gallagher made me swear not to tell anybody. You'll just have to wait and see for yourself, because Gallagher said if I told anyone, he'd spread liverwurst on my tongue.

1 MARCH—DAY 146

Dear Wenny,

I screwed up really badly. And it was all because I wanted to make a cake for your birthday. Mum didn't have any cake mix, so I had to use what I could. I took my stash of Snickers bars down from the cupboard shelf and counted them. There were nine in all. That's a lot to give up for you.

While Mum was at the shops, I melted the bars in a pan on the cooker. It looked pretty gloppy for cake, so I went to get some flour. Bullwinkle ran into me while I was carrying the bag. Some flour spilled on his back; it made him look like he had the world's worst case of dog dandruff. Some more flour got on the floor, but there was still a lot in the bag.

I poured some onto the melted Snickers bar and stirred the pot. I have to tell you, it smelled pretty good. Some chocolate got on the counter when I laid the spoon down, but I was good about it. I did-n't lick it off the counter or anything. I wiped it up with a napkin.

Bullwinkle snarfed the napkin out of my hand. I had to chase him around the house because dogs aren't supposed to have chocolate. It can make a dog sick. We left flour footprints and pawprints on the rugs everywhere we ran. Before I could catch him, Bullwinkle showed me how smart he is by eat-ing the whole paper napkin. I mean it. He ate it.

By the time I got back to the kitchen, the cake mix was burning a little, so I poured some water into the pan and stirred some more. I wanted to get the burned taste out of the chocolate, so I dumped in some strawberry jam. That usually works pretty well on burned toast. Next I heated up the oven and got out the cake pan.

I poured the mix into the cake pan without spilling very much. I decided to decorate the top so it would look really professional. There was a bag of marshmallow treats in the cupboard. Some were blue and shaped like stars. Some were yellow half-moon shapes. Perfect. First I made a circle of blue stars on top of the cake, then I added a few yellow moons. The cake looked really good, even though it was still raw.

I felt so good about myself I ate a couple of marshmallows.

I was licking the spoon when Mum came in.

"William Alan North! What in the world are you doing?" She thumped her grocery bag on the counter and put her hands on her hips.

"I'm making a cake."

"Who told you you could make a cake?"

"You did."

"I did not!"

"You did. Last year at Wenny's birthday party I said I wanted to make her a cake, and you said I could when she turned eight."

Mum's mouth fell open. Her whole body started to shake. I got her a glass of water. She sat down on a kitchen chair and stared at the flour on the floor. She didn't even touch her water. "I'll sweep up the flour," I said. "I'll sweep it up right now."

I cleaned the kitchen so well you wouldn't even know I tried to make a cake. I dusted the flour off my trainers and washed the bottoms of Bullwinkle's feet so he wouldn't make any more white pawprints. I vacuumed his prints and mine off the rugs.

Mum put away the groceries and went to her room to lie down. I wish I could make Mum better. I'm always screwing up. She's always going to her room and closing the door.

Okay, so the cake didn't turn out so well, but Gallagher and I have better plans. You'll find out about it soon. I can't tell you what they are yet because I hate the taste of liverwurst.

Chapter 33

2 MARCH—DAY 147

Surprise, Wenny!

I bet you didn't think you'd be getting any presents this year. Well, I wouldn't go and forget something as important as your birthday. I sent you a card, but I thought I'd write this letter, too, and tell you all the stuff we did.

First of all, Gallagher and I headed for the woods this afternoon with all your presents. Bullwinkle ran ahead to sniff out the trail. We must have looked pretty stupid hiking through the trees with a bunch of helium balloons tied to our belts, but nobody saw us, so that's okay.

It ended up taking us more than two hours to find the meadow Gallagher was looking for. Even though my cast has been off for more than two months, my leg started to get sore from all that walking. By three o'clock I was ready to kill Gallagher because I thought we were lost. But we finally made it to the meadow, and so we got all happy again.

Bullwinkle ran around in circles while we got out your party stuff. We didn't have a cake, but we brought six chocolate marshmallow bars, and they were pretty good. Bullwinkle didn't feel left out because he chewed a Milk-Bone.

After Gallagher chomped down his third marshmallow bar, he licked his teeth and said, "Time for presents."

I fished in the bag for the new red gumball ring I've been saving in my box. I tied it on a yellow balloon with the rest of your gumball rings. The rings are pretty light because they're made of plastic. All your presents had to be light this year because helium balloons can't carry much.

Next we tied Bullwinkle's present on to the pink and green balloons. He thought you'd like Twinkie's kitty snake. Twinkie didn't want it any more with all the catnip shaken out of it. But Bullwinkle's been pretty attached to it, so I hope you tell him thank you.

Next we sent off Gallagher's presents. He's pretty proud of that photograph of himself blowing the big bubble. Did you know it takes six pieces of bubble gum to make a bubble that huge? He also thought you'd like the picture he drew of Godzilla with his arm around his girlfriend, the Statue of Liberty.

We didn't sing "Happy Birthday," but I taught Gallagher how to sing your made-up song, "Alligator Jam". He liked the part that goes, "Squish the jam between your toes. Stick the jam up your nose."

I tied the last present on four red balloons because my magnet is pretty heavy, even though the horseshoe part of it is made of plastic. I sent the card, too. I hope you like my picture of the light person.

P.S. I want you to take good care of my magnet, Wenny. Don't go losing it on some cloud or anything. You can be sure my magnet will never lose its power because it's real.

DAY 147 (STILL)

Dear Wenny,

We never should have trusted Bullwinkle. He's got the brains of a mosquito! The sun was already setting when we left the meadow, so we knew we had to hurry.

After walking through the woods for a while, Bullwinkle ran down another trail. Then he came back barking his head off.

"I think he's found a short cut," said Gallagher.

"So?"

"So, I think we should follow him."

"No way," I said.

"If we don't, we'll be walking home in the dark," said Gallagher. "We should cut across the woods like Bullwinkle says."

"Did Bullwinkle say all that?"

"No, he just found a short cut. Come on."

Like two totally deranged dumbheads, we followed Bullwinkle! He took us on a smaller trail. It's what Gallagher calls a deer trail because animals make it instead of people. Gallagher said deer trails are good because animals know where they're going. When the trail got steep, Gallagher said that was a good sign. We'd get out of the hills faster and down into the flat part of the forest that leads into town. That was before the deer trail jerked around and started going uphill again.

Well, we started following Bullwinkle around five-thirty. Now it's seven-thirty. Gallagher's down at the stream getting us some water. I'm sitting here in the moonlight, freezing my butt off while I write this letter.

Once we realized the deer trail was a stupid plan, we got to work searching for the people trail again. That was an hour ago. We've walked through tons of underbrush in the moonlight. The deer trail doesn't connect up to the people trail anywhere we can find. Bottom line, someone's going to have to come after us if we're going to get out of here tonight because we're l-o-s-t, lost. The only one who's happy is Bullwinkle and that's because he's too stupid to be scared.

We don't have a torch, or sleeping bags, or normal overnight stuff. But Gallagher found a stream so we won't be thirsty. Gallagher says he knows all about survival in the woods because he's a Scout. He brought a half box of crackers and a funny kind of tube with peanut butter inside of it. You squeeze the peanut butter out just like toothpaste. I know you hate peanut butter, Wenny, but it tastes pretty darn good when you're stuck in the middle of nowhere at dinnertime.

I'm glad we brought our coats. I'm glad Bullwinkle is curled up next to me. His breath is warm on my hands. Gallagher's coming back with the water now so I've got to stop writing. Watch over us tonight, Wenny. I think we'll need it.

Chapter 34

Dear Wenny,

Night came on fast. I was glad we had a full moon, or the forest would have been completely dark. Stars are nice to look at, but they don't give off any more light than a bunch of fireflies, which is to say they don't give off any.

I've never been so cold. Not even on that rainy day when I was locked out of the house and had to wait two hours in the tree house for Mum to get

213

back from shopping. My feet are the most cold. I've been worried about frostbite, but Gallagher said I should just keep wiggling my toes inside my shoes. I've been doing that, but it doesn't help much.

Bullwinkle may be stupid. He may have got us lost. But it's hard to be angry with him, because he's been doing a good job keeping us warm. Gallagher and I have been taking turns lying next to Bullwinkle. We've been covering ourselves with redwood branches. It's kind of like sleeping with a porcupine blanket.

When I get a little bit warmed up, Gallagher lies down in the middle, and we fix up the branches again. We've been switching places all night, which means I've hardly got any sleep.

The only one who's been sleeping much is Bullwinkle. Not only that, he doesn't seem to be cold at all. A fur coat is better than skin, I've decided. God should have made us that way so we wouldn't have to get so cold when we're outside. I think you should talk to Him about it next time you see Him.

Well, I'm going to curl up beside Gallagher some more. I can't sleep, but I can't write any more, either. My hands are too cold outside my coat sleeves. My teeth are starting to chatter. I want this night to be over right now.

DAY 148

Dear Wenny,

It was Dad who found us. He must have a talent for finding people, because lots of people were searching for us in the wrong places all night long, even the police! Dad spent most of the night checking everywhere he could think of in town, then he decided to try the woods. He reached the trail at about five in the morning. Clouds rolled in and it had started to rain. Dad walked and shouted and walked and shouted.

As soon as we heard him, we shouted back and started running. Dad raced through the mud and picked me up and held me tight. "I thought I'd lost you!" he cried.

Even though it was raining and the wind was blowing hard, I felt Dad's arms around me. He didn't let me go for a long time. His big arms sent warmth through my whole body.

Before we headed back, Dad used his mobile phone to call off the search. He told everyone he was taking us back to our house.

When we walked through the front door, Mum and Gallagher's family were there waiting with a policeman. Everybody hugged and cried. Gallagher's mum told us we were wet and cold, which we already knew. Mum said we were hun-gry, and we knew that, too. Pretty soon we were wrapped in wool blankets. We sat on the couch chomping down scrambled eggs and stacks of toast with but-ter and strawberry jam.

The policeman sat across from us in Dad's big chair. "I just need to ask you boys a few questions," he said. "What were you doing in the woods?"

I finished my glass of orange juice. "Walking," I said.

"We got lost," said Gallagher.

"Duh!" I said.

"What time did you head out yesterday?" asked the cop.

"About one o'clock," I said.

Gallagher jammed a hunk of toast in his mouth. "We had a lot of stuff to get together before we could go."

"Hiking gear?" asked the cop.

"Birthday-party stuff," said Gallagher. I poked him in the side.

The cop leaned forward. "Which one of you is having a birthday?" he asked.

"Neither one of us," said Gallagher. "It was Wenny's birthday."

Dad sucked in his breath.

I wanted to strangle Gallagher.

"Wenny," said the cop. He wrote it down on his clipboard. "Was there another kid with you out there? I thought only you two boys were missing."

"It was just us," I said.

"Then who's Wenny?"

Dad left the room. I could hear the water running in the kitchen. Mum sat down next to me on the couch. "Wenny was our daughter," she said. "She died in October."

Chapter 35

Dear Wenny,

After everybody left, I started to notice a stink. I sniffed my clothes and decided it was me. That's what I get for sleeping next to Bullwinkle.

Remember Mr Big Bubble? I poured a whole cup into the bath. That bath felt so good. It smelled good, too. I stayed inside a mountain of bubbles till I was warm all the way into my bones. Then I dressed and went down the hall.

Mum and Dad were standing by the kitchen sink. They were hugging. They didn't see me, because I was outside the door.

Dad was saying, "Sorry, Kate." Mum was touching Dad's cheek where it was rough from not shaving. I sneaked back down the hall and lay down on my bed. I hadn't seen them hug like that for a long time. I didn't want to get in their way.

DAY 152

Dear Wenny,

It's been a couple of days since Gallagher and I got lost. Here's what's going on. First of all, you should know that Mum and Dad are still seeing Mrs Kershel at the Family Counselling Centre. I think they'll be seeing her for a long time, but Dad has moved back into our house, and that's something to be glad about.

This afternoon I climbed up to our tree house. I hadn't been up there since Mr James carried me up the ladder. The floor of the tree house was a mess. Dead leaves were everywhere. They were all wet and brown, like soggy cornflakes. I wanted to make the tree house nice again, so I took the broom up and started to sweep.

I was working up a sweat by the time Dad came outside.

"Hey, Dad."

"What are you going to do with those leaves?" he asked.

"Dump them over the edge."

"Wait," said Dad. He went into the house and came back with a dustpan and bin-bag sack. He climbed right up to the tree house. My skin got prickly just having him up there with me. He hasn't been in the tree house since our water-balloon fight last summer.

Dad bent down with the dustpan and started shoveling brown leaves into the bin-bag. I kept sweeping. The broom uncovered a piece of red rubber. Dad picked up the balloon skin. "This one hit me in the face," he said.

"Wenny was a good shot," I said.

Dad rubbed the balloon with his thumb. "She was good at lots of things," he said. His head was

221

bent down so I could see the grey hairs on his head.

"She could make you laugh," I said.

Dad wiped some dirt from his hands. I kept talking.

"It wasn't your fault," I said.

The branch above us creaked in the wind. Dad looked up at me through his glasses. "I shouldn't have let you go to town," he said.

"Why not? We'd walked to the craft store lots of times before."

Dad was on his knees by the leaf bag. I was standing above him. I could have touched the top of his head, if I'd wanted to.

"I should have driven you," he said.

"We wanted to walk."

Dad put down his dustpan. Then he stood up and leaned against the banister. I stepped up next to him. He was breathing hard. Some wind came along and blew the leaves off the top of our pile. It was almost like he was making the wind from his own mouth. A few leaves twirled in the air and flew over the garden fence.

"It's been almost five months," said Dad.

"It's been one hundred and fifty-two days," I said.

"You've been counting?"

"I've been counting."

Dad put his arm around me. We looked out over the neighbourhood rooftops. "Things will never be the same," he said.

"I know."

We watched the wind blow thick clouds across the whole sky, but the sun broke through in some places.

Chapter 36

Dear Wenny,

The world is supposed to end on 9 March at six o'clock. Lots of important psychics have predicted it. Since today is 8 March, Gallagher brought his sister's *Extravaganza* magazine to school today and showed everyone the "World Will End!" headline. He scared most of the kids on the playground. One kid peed his pants. When Mrs Terwilliger found out, she locked the *Extravaganza* magazine in her desk and made Gallagher sit in the corner near the science shelf. He spent most of the day visiting Igor's exoskeleton.

9 MARCH—DAY 154 (PSYCHICS SAY THE WORLD ENDS TODAY!)

Dear Wenny,

When I got home from Gallagher's house this afternoon, Mum was putting a new cot together in your room. There were big empty cardboard boxes on your floor with crib parts sticking out of them. Mum was on her hands and knees, reading a page of instructions.

The paint on your walls has been dry for a long time now, so Mum has moved some stuff back in. She put your two shelves back against the wall. One shelf is full of baby toys and stacks of clean nappies. The other shelf has your stuff on it.

It made me feel good to see some of your things back in your room. Mum put Milton bear on the top shelf next to the catapult you made. I picked up the catapult and tested the rubber band. You did a good job, because it still works.

I went to my room and took the ballerina out of my cupboard. I've been keeping her safe for you there. I took her back to your room and put her on the top shelf next to Milton. Mum looked up. I couldn't tell if the ballerina made her happy or sad, because she had a screw sticking out of her mouth.

"Come over here and hold this," she said around the screw. I held up two sides of the cot and she put the screw in the hole. We worked on the cot for a while, then I heard the front door slam.

I was handing Mum the screwdriver when Dad came into your room. He patted the green blanket on the baby's shelf. Then he looked at the clay handprint you made for him in nursery school. He reached out for it, but his hand stayed in the air.

Mum finished tightening the last screw. Now the cot had four sides. She let out a big breath and stood up slowly.

"Can you guys help me out?" she said. Dad

turned around. Mum rubbed her big belly. "I need the mattress and bedsprings from the garage."

"Okay," said Dad.

I followed Dad to the garage. He grabbed the springs leaning against the wall. "What do you think?" he asked.

"About what?"

"About having a new baby in the house."

"I'm glad about it," I said. I wanted to tell him it was pretty hard work being the only kid in a family, but I wasn't sure how he'd take it, so I said, "It'll be fun."

Dad and I lifted the springs together. The metal springs hurt my hands. We walked down the hall really carefully so we wouldn't scratch the walls.

"Alley-oop," said Dad as we hefted the springs over the side of the cot. "Okay, now let it down real slow," said Dad. "Good."

Next we got the mattress and lowered it down on to the springs. The crib was all done except for sheets and stuff. We all stepped back by the pile of cardboard, plastic bags and instruction sheets.

"Looks nice," said Mum. She ran her hand across the back of Dad's neck. "Thanks, honey."

Dad gave her a kiss. We decided to have some pizza and clean up the mess later.

DAY 154 (STILL)

Dear Wenny,

After dinner we all went back to work in your room. I jammed used-up paper and bits of string into my plastic bin-bag. Mum put away the tools. Dad crushed the cardboard boxes flat. He always gets that job because he has the biggest feet.

Dad stomped on another box, then he looked around the room. "Good paint job," he said.

"Will chose the colours," said Mum.

Dad pointed to the wall above the cot, where I'd put a hole in the clouds. "Missed a spot," he said.

I shook my head. "No, I didn't."

Dad gave me a funny look.

"I wanted the baby to know where Wenny is," I said.

Mum put her hand to her mouth. I started to get

that roller-coaster feeling in my stomach. I knew I was going to tell them now. Mr James wasn't here to help me. I had to do this by myself. I would just tell them the good part about flying. "I died in the hospital when the doctors were trying to fix me."

Mum nodded really slowly. "We know. The doctor told us that when you came out of surgery."

"Well," I said. "What you don't know is that when I died, something big happened to me. I floated up out of my body and I flew through a dark tunnel. Then I saw Wenny flying up ahead of me in a river of light."

Dad put his arm around Mum. "This is a dream you had," he said.

"No," I said. "It's what happened when I died. Wenny and I were zooming through the sky. It was really bright and colourful, and the light was all inside of me, like I'd swallowed it."

"You saw Wenny?" whispered Mum.

"Yeah, but she flew ahead of me with the light person. I wanted to go with her, but I started thinking about you both being alone down in the world.

All of a sudden I was back at the hospital, kind of floating in the corner of the ceiling. I saw you both in the waiting room. I tried to talk to you and tell you I was all right, but you couldn't hear me.

"Dad, I saw you knock over that paper cup and spill the water. Mum bent down to wipe up the water, and you got down on your knees. You were both crying. You put your arms around Mum and you said . . ."

I stopped talking and dropped my bin-bag on the floor. I hadn't meant to tell that part of the story. Not the waiting-room part. I was just going to say I'd seen Wenny. She was okay. She was happy.

"Said what, Will?"

I wanted to crawl inside the bin-bag and curl up with the orange peels and pizza crusts and little bits of string.

"What did you hear me say?"

"You said . . . 'Why did it have to be Wenny?'"

The room went all quiet. My heart was bashing in my chest like a hammer.

Then Dad sucked in a big breath, like he'd just swum up from the bottom of the ocean. "Will," he said. He put his hands on my shoulders. I didn't want to look at his face, but when I did, I saw blotches of colour on his cheekbones. "You mean you thought I wished you were killed instead of Wenny?" He shook his head. "No," he whispered. "I didn't want either one of you to die. Not my girl," he said. "And not my boy."

He pulled me close. Mum came over and wrapped her arms around us, and we were all crying.

We stood in the middle of your room. I was right in the middle of both of them, and it was the whole centre of the world.

"I thought you wanted Wenny," I said. "But I still came back."

Mum rubbed my neck. Dad ran his hand across my head. "Thanks for coming back," he said.

DAY 154 (LATER)

Dear Wenny,

It's almost eight o'clock and the world didn't come to an end. I think those psychics need to take some remedial maths classes.

It took me almost five months to fill up this book, but I'm on the last page, so this is my last letter to you for a while. I'm glad now I told Mum and Dad the whole story. It's good to know I was wrong about what Dad said in the waiting room that day. It's also good for Mom and Dad to know where you are, so they won't worry so much.

I'm not angry with you anymore for flying ahead of me. I know you were just happy to be zooming around up there. We didn't make it all the way across the street on this world. I couldn't stop that truck. But I did fly you some of the way to heaven. I got you far enough along the bright road to see that nice light person, so I guess I did my job.

Thank you for being your crazy, happy self. For playing with me when there was no one else around and for singing me all those weird made-up songs.

I want you to remember, no matter how many zillion angel friends you make up there, I want you to remember that I'm still your big brother.

Love,

Will